DANI'S Inferno

SCOTT M. RUTHERFORD

Inspirational. Positive. Encouraging.

DANI'S INFERNO
By Scott M. Rutherford
Published by TouchPoint Faith
(a TouchPoint Press imprint)
Brookland, AR 72417
www.touchpointpress.com

ISBN-13: 978-1-952816-13-0

Scriptures taken from *The Holy Bible, New International Version*. Grand Rapids: Zondervan Publishing House, 1984 and *The Holy Bible: King James Version*. Dallas, TX: Brown Books Publishing, 2004.

Lyrics from "Daring to Dream" used with permission. Copyright One True King (1TK). Visit 1Tk online https://1tkband.com/

Editor: Ashley Carlson
Cover Design: Tricia Rutherford and Colbie Myles

First Edition

Printed in the United States of America.

To my firstborn, AC, who challenged me to finally write it

Chapter One

Rio Flaco, California
Friday, January 11, 1991

Smoke, sweat, and Aqua Net assaulted seventeen-year-old Dani Grassigli as she opened the garage's side door. Doing her best to ignore the Mötley Crüe knockoff providing the noise, she stood tiptoe, scanning gaps in the jungle of teased hair for a glimpse of her best friend, Shelly. *Shouldn't be here. Vic finds out, I'm dead. And if Daddy finds out…*

Some guy from last year's chemistry class backed into her, laughed, and offered a joint.

Dani shook her head, trying to ignore him as he traced her figure with his eyes. She knew her floral jeans and button up blouse weren't racy. *What do I have to do to get them to stop? Dress like a nun?*

She kept her head down and elbowed her way to the corner where the band—Inferno, according to the double bass drumheads—struck up a sappy power ballad heavy on the oohs, aahs, and babies. Bobby Van Zie, Shelly's new boyfriend, kicked into the obligatory guitar solo, shaking his bleached mane and snarling for the crowd.

Oh wow, sweeping arpeggios. Dani rolled her eyes. *Cliché much? But is that a Les Paul he's playing?* "No time to drool," Dani reminded herself. *Looks like a '68. Sunburst.*

Shelly perched on the edge of a tattered couch across the stage, eyes glued to Bobby as she swayed in time. A paunchy guy with a bald spot at the crown of his mullet slouched on the other end of the couch. He inched closer, eyes alternating between the hem of Shelly's miniskirt and his watch.

I told her not to wear that. Dani stepped between them, yelling over the music. "She's with the guitar player!"

"What guitar player?" Paunchy reclined, giving Dani the once-over.

"C'mon, Shel, we gotta go." Dani tugged her by the elbow.

"But this is our song. Just till it's over?"

"We get caught here, we're dead!" Dani said, turning her back to Paunchy and sniffing the collar of her shirt. "You have any idea what Vic will do if I show up smelling like pot?"

Shelly rolled her eyes. "Not like he's your dad."

"Don't go there," Dani bit her lip to keep from tearing up. "Besides, he's my boss."

"He's your brother," Shelly mouthed, smirking.

"What if someone from church sees us? I'll get kicked off the praise team!" *And we'd never hear the end of it in youth group.*

Shelly laughed. "Here?"

Paunchy scooched closer, leaning in. The song's crescendo drowned his words, but his meaning was clear. He drummed his fingers and jingled his Cadillac keychain, flashing his Rolex.

Dani pulled Shelly off the couch, turning to face the man as the last notes faded. "Don't know what you're selling, but we're not buying. Hey Shelly, let's—"

Shelly had already jumped up onto the stage, giggling and whispering into Bobby's ear. The two heads melded into one mass of bleach blond hair until Bobby pulled away and winked at the rest of the band.

"You can be replaced," the singer said into the microphone, drawing laughter from the crowd as Shelly led Bobby out by the hand.

Dani took a second look at the singer. Vince Neil hair. Bon Jovi smile. Looked like he stepped off the pages of Hit Parader. *No time to dwell on that, of all things.* "I ought to just leave you here!"

Shelly turned in the doorway. "Five minutes?" The door slammed, and the couple was gone before Dani could answer.

The partiers groaned their unanimous sentiment at the interruption.

Wonder if they've seen that trick before?

"Jump!" The singer hollered, looking desperate to stem the flow heading for the door.

The bass player stepped behind a keyboard rig and started plunking out the opening riff to the Van Halen song as what was left of the band fell in.

The '68 Gibson lay on the stage floor next to the amp, calling Dani's name.

Guy has no idea what he's got. Dani looked at a wall clock. Four-thirty. *And he's bad for Shelly. Betcha he won't like it if—* She stretched out over the stage, snagging the guitar and strapping it on as the singer belted:

"I ain't the worst that you've seen…"

"Sure ain't," Dani said, trying to catch his eye as she pulled the pick from between the strings, cranked the volume knob to make sure Bobby could hear from outside and hit the fill leading into the chorus. The fretboard fit her hand like a buttered glove, and the amplifiers growled a warning. *This is going to get dangerous.* Dani locked in with the bass player through the chorus as if she'd been rehearsing with the band for months. The singer dropped his jaw as his mic hit the floor with a dull thud. By the time she nailed the finger-tap solo, he retrieved it and stumbled through the rest of the song.

In another garage across town, Vic Grassigli paced between a '67 Mustang fastback that looked like it had just rolled off the assembly line and a '70 Superbird that looked like it had rolled over a land mine.

Greg, the shop's chief mechanic, worked under the Plymouth, greasy boots protruding. "Not my turn to watch your sister."

"Like that's ever stopped you before," Vic said.

The Marine Corps anchor and shield on the wall clock's face made it hard to read from across the room, but Vic knew five o'clock approached. *Opportunities like this don't come every day.*

Greg emerged, wiping his wrenches with a shop cloth until they gleamed. His coveralls shared a logo with Vic's: "Fidelis Classic Restoration" superimposed over a Firebird image just distinct enough from Pontiac's to avoid a lawsuit. Not that you could read it, covered in every automotive fluid known to man plus mustard.

Greg knew why Vic was staring. Greg always knew. "You want the reporter to think nobody works around here?" Greg said.

"Not paying you to argue with me." Vic forced a smile. "Just finish and clean up a little, will you?"

"Which?" Greg called after him as Vic retreated into the glassed-in office.

Sitting at the steel desk his father had picked up at a military surplus store, Vic took a deep breath and sent up a prayer, doing his best not to get worked up over Dani being late. Again.

This whole thing's tougher on her than it is on me, with Dad halfway around the world.

He fingered a Polaroid taped to the window. The family on the chapel steps at Quantico, right around the time they had started attending church regularly. *Seven years ago.* Seemed like longer. He was sixteen then. Dani was all elbows, curls, and teeth. Mom wouldn't have her hair much longer, but she had it then. It was almost impossible to tell from the picture that she was already sick. Dad wore his dress blues, twenty years' worth of ribbons and medals pinned to his chest. It wasn't long after that he'd switched to the Reserves and moved the family here.

"Dani wouldn't push her limits like this if you were home," Vic said, trying to come up with reasons to give her the benefit of the doubt. "Maybe she just forgot."

He called home. Mom's voice on the answering machine. No one in the family could bring themselves to change it. He dialed another number. Kari, the church's youth and worship leader, hadn't seen her. He tried Shelly's house.

The crowd roared as the guitar screamed the final lick. Dani gave it a shake, squeezing every drop from the fading note. Electricity mingled with guilt coursed through her. Images of her father halfway around the world flashed through her brain, his smile fading to a tight-lipped stare that came as close to a frown as she'd ever seen on his face.

She shook her head as the singer flourished his hand. "All right! That's…?"

Bluest eyes I've ever seen.

The singer shrugged, gesturing toward an open mic.

Ooh, dimples. Dani shrugged back, drawing a laugh. *Any other time, any other place.*

The bass player leaned over and whispered something into the singer's ear. *Don't I know him?* He looked about her age, a little younger than the singer.

"That's Dani Grass!" the singer said with a flourish toward her.

Dimples ignored Don't-I-Know-Him's attempt to correct him.

Just as well. Last thing I need is my name getting around in a place like this.

Turning to Dani, Dimples mouthed, "One more?"

Dani looked over at the clock. It looked like the hands had barely moved. *Not every day I get my hands on a '68 Les Paul.* Shelly wasn't back yet, anyway. Shrugging, she said, "What can it hurt?" and laid into the opening licks of "Sweet Child O' Mine."

5

Guy sounds almost as good as Axl, and he's a lot better looking. The crowd faded as their eyes met. *He's smiling. At me.* Dani looked at the floor, felt herself biting her lip. *Man-that-looks-stupid-don't-do-that.*

A minute and a half in, almost done with the first solo, she looked back at the drummer. He had to be at least five years older than the singer, who she figured was in his early twenties. *This song's like five minutes long. Bad pick, Dani.*

Paunchy Mullet caught the corner of her eye as he pulled himself off the couch and slunk to the stage. Staring. *Gross.* She turned away from him and glanced to make sure her blouse was buttoned as she kicked into the second solo. *About two minutes left.* Time for overdrive. *That clock still hasn't moved. At all.*

"...Where do we go? Where do we go now?"

She stole a glimpse at her Swatch. *I'm so dead. Minute and change left in the song and then I gotta hit the door running, even if I have to drag Shelly.*

❝Really think you should wait and let Dani handle that," Greg said as he headed to the bathroom.

"Take care of your business and let me take care of mine," Vic said. Dani's habit of showing up when she felt like it had messed up enough for one day. And this project was on a ticking clock. *May not be the artist Dani is, but I can handle a pinstripe.*

With inches to go, Vic took a deep breath and admired his work. A flash of burnt orange caught his eye, and he flinched, throwing the stripe off course as the rapid-fire ping-ping-ping of gravel against the metal siding announced the arrival of Dani's GTO. Uttering something between a cuss word and a prayer, he threw the pinstriping tool against the wall.

Greg picked up the remains of the tool as he stepped from the bathroom. "New detailing technique, Boss?"

Vic slammed his palm against the Mustang's hood. He closed his eyes, reminding himself, "Wisdom yields patience; it is to a man's glory to overlook an offense." Truth be told, he knew he wasn't a good enough mechanic to run the place without Greg. *Be tough to replace him, even though Dad's known for his overly generous payroll.* He looked back at the car. "Think anyone'll notice?"

"She'll notice."

"She won't—"

His kid sister rushed in, leaving the door swinging, apology written all over her face.

"Second time's not a mistake," Vic said. "Much less the seventeenth in a month."

Dani groaned and rushed to the fastback, her eyes demanding an explanation as she ran her finger along the errant stripe. "Talk about mistakes."

She's trying to turn the tables. Like always. "Mr. Wilkins is on a plane."

"Next time you want to help…"

Vic gritted his teeth. "We can't afford to lose his business."

"At least the news lady stopped by," Greg said as he stepped between them.

"And chatted with me and Greasy McGee instead of getting a story about a brother and sister carrying on the family business while daddy's off getting ready to rescue Kuwait," Vic said. "Semper Fi. Oorah. Red, white, and blue, and all that."

Greg stiffened.

"Who knows if they'll even show it now." Vic slumped against a tool case. "Would've been great publicity."

"Corps means a lot more to Gunny than News at Eleven."

Don't I know it? Dad had always spent more time with his Marines than his kids. Greg was the third injured Marine his father had employed since opening the shop. "Mr. Wilkins expects his car in the morning."

"Maybe I can fix it." Dani knelt by the side panel, squinting. "Where's the pinstriper?"

That night, Dani clung to Teddy Bear, her oversized Chow Chow. The dog stood sentry as she sobbed into his black mane. Vic rehearsed excuses for Mr. Wilkins' car not being finished outside her door. Loudly. Greg sped down the highway—on the clock, Vic had reminded her—somewhere between here and LA. He wouldn't get any sleep tonight, but he would get a lot of overtime, and she'd have the tools she needed by sunrise.

On the other side of the world, Daddy would be waking up. She could hear him praying for her and Vic, like he had every morning since she was ten, three hours before her alarm went off. She'd always loved waking up that way.

Daddy was counting on her now. Vic didn't have the touch she'd picked up from Daddy for resurrecting rusty classics. He ran the business end well enough. He'd always been more like their mother. Best she could tell, the only thing Dani had inherited from their mother was her curls. "Thanks a lot for that," she'd often said while torturing herself with hairbrushes. Everyone else said they wished they had her curls. Everyone else didn't have to deal with them.

She opened her closet and filed through to the white lace dress in the back, running the sash through her fingers like she often did when she was stressed or found herself missing Mom. She hoped someday she'd look as pretty in it as Mom had in the wedding picture that hung above the family's mantle.

The last time she'd talked alone with Mom, she'd promised she'd save herself for that night, though at the time, she hadn't been too clear about what she was saving. She fiddled with the purity ring Kari had given out in youth group last month. "I'm a mess, but at least I'm still good as far as that goes." *Someday I'll trade it for Mom's ring.*

She wiped tears on her sleeve.

Dani sat and reached for her acoustic guitar on the other end of the closet.

Teddy Bear ambled over, blocking the door, as she quietly fingerpicked. Music made sense, even when nothing else in the world did.

"And while I'm trying to figure out how to avoid losing our shirts, she's playing 'Don't Worry, Be Happy!'"

Dani stopped, sure she wasn't meant to hear that.

"Rome's burning! Nero's fiddling!"

Okay, that was meant for me.

"She's trying. God, give me patience with her. I don't know how I'm going to make it through this."

It's my fault Vic's freaking out. Wish Mom was here. She'd be able to calm him down.

The phone rang. Daddy didn't usually call on Fridays, but if he did, it would be about now. Dani hurdled Teddy Bear and tossed her guitar on the bed in a rush to beat Vic to the phone.

But it was Kari, calling to tell her she'd have to sit out of the praise band for a couple weeks.

"I only missed one practice." Dani bit her lip. "And I told you ahead of time."

"That you'd be at work."

No point arguing. Kari didn't let just anyone up front, no matter how talented and no matter how big a crush she had on their older brother. Not during youth group and especially not on Sunday. *Just glad she doesn't know where I was. I'd never play again.* Dani resigned herself to the sermon to follow. *At least she cares.*

Kari was just getting wound up on faithfulness in little things and knowing to do good and not doing it when call waiting saved Dani from the big finish about obeying those in authority.

Please, God, let it be important enough so I can tell Kari I'll call her back.

Shelly wanting to get their stories straight in case her mom talked to Dani.

Close enough.

Chapter Two

Sometime after midnight, Dani sat in the garage, toying with the steering wheel of Daddy's other baby. There were only eight like it—four, if you considered the two transmission options.

She remembered when Daddy first saw it. She was six or seven then. She could still smell the musty barn where he'd found it, a rusty heap. She could hear the break in the voices of the silver-haired couple talking with Daddy.

She'd never seen Daddy cry before. Or since.

She'd since learned that Private First Class Daniel Jenkins parked it there in '71.

She'd heard Daddy tell the story so many times that she knew the details by heart. Daddy had carried his buddy and laid him in a medivac chopper at Quang Tri.

Daddy had wanted to look up Jenkins' parents for years. By the time business brought him close enough to the Michigan state line to do it, he had to force himself. He'd brought Dani along so she could learn a little about the man she was named after.

Over the next few years, Daddy took as many trips as he could out to the Michigan farm country. Sometimes, Dani got to go. They were making the car like new, Daddy said, because Danny would have liked that.

Dani smiled, knowing she must have been underfoot at the time. Daddy would bark instructions at her in that Marine Corps drill instructor tone that always meant "I love you" to her ears. To hear Daddy tell it, he couldn't have done the job without her. She remembered him letting her turn the key, that growl under the hood, and the beams in Daddy's eyes when it first saw the light of day.

Daddy never expected the couple to give him the title.

She knew he'd had offers as high as a quarter million for the car, but the 1969 ½ Trans Am rested right where Dani sat in it now, venturing out only for an occasional car show or parade.

Who knows? Maybe if Daddy had sold it, no one would have discovered his talent for bringing rust buckets back from the dead. Maybe he wouldn't have invested his life savings in starting the shop. Maybe he'd have just served his twenty years and got out three years ago, with no need to continue in the Reserves. He'd be retired, and someone else's dad would be in danger halfway around the world.

At least they're not fighting yet. Daddy had said it wasn't likely mechanics would be close to any heavy fighting, anyhow, even if what they were calling Operation Desert Shield did come to war. And Vic told her he'd seen on the news the Iraqi missiles were outdated and unlikely to hit much anyway.

Still, it only takes one.

Dani lay her head on the wheel. "Daddy, I know he's right to be mad." That news story would have been a huge deal for Fidelis Restoration, and it didn't even air.

She yawned.

ani jolted awake at the squeak of the house door and squinted against the dusk. Vic stretched the phone cord as far as it could reach, as he sat on the garage steps and closed the door, taking pains not to let it slam.

"I know it's early." Vic's voice hovered just above a whisper. "But playing with the worship band means everything to her."

Dani melted into the seat.

"...look, I get it... but it's been tough getting her to even come to church since... listen, she's going through... will you just think about it?" A pause, a sigh. "Tonight? Yeah, I guess I could."

An hour later, as the last shades of red kissed the horizon good morning, Dani parked next to Greg's beat-up Chevy, Greg's snoring face smushed against the window. The new pinstriping kit waited on the bench seat.

Where'd he find a Beugler in the middle of the night?

"Shhhhhh," Dani said, as if the groaning hinges could hear.

Greg shook, ran his hands through his stubble, and blinked his bloodshot green eyes repeatedly.

"Go get some sleep," Dani said.

"Might as well work." He yawned and stretched. "I'm wide awake."

Dani considered her 0-for-lifetime record arguing with Marines. She didn't have time to try improving on it today. As it was, she'd have to work faster than she liked for a job that was going to take finesse. And a little luck.

Vic stretched breakfast with Ed Wilkins as long as he could. No, Mr. Wilkins didn't want to see the sites.

"Headed straight from the shop to Highway 1."

No, he didn't need to stop anywhere. Not even the bank.

"Check's right here," Mr. Wilkins said, patting the breast of his sports coat. "Just need the keys. Have to admit, I half expected a call, what with your old man away."

"I run a tight ship." *If Dani doesn't sink it.*

Vic took the long way. Caught every yellow light he could. *Twenty more minutes and we're there. No way she's had enough time.*

Mr. Wilkins drummed his fingers. "If the job's the quality I've come to expect from your dad, I've got two more lined up—'57 Chevys."

"We can handle them," Vic said, mind racing for anything to stall just a little longer.

"Need the right touch."

"Have we failed you yet?" Vic said, pulling into an Exxon station. "Need to hit the men's room."

"Man, I'd love to be in your business," Mr. Wilkins said to himself as both stepped out of the car.

At the shop, Dani forced herself to ignore the clock as she did what she could with the botched stripe. *Can only polish a turd so much.*

"I don't think you need to worry about it." Greg let out a satisfied grunt as he broke something loose under the Superbird in the next bay.

"Easy for you to say. Vic spent half the night hollering about how this is our best client."

"He couldn't run this place without you." Greg slid out from underneath the car and sat up on the creeper. "And he knows it."

"Wouldn't trade places for anything. Can you picture me trying to deal with people?"

"I can picture it."

Dani stepped back and scrunched her face as she eyed the work from several angles. "Mr. What's-His-Face is not gonna like this." There was no way to fix Vic's mistake without stripping the paint and starting over. Dani had done her best to work the splotch into a design – something that at least looked intentional.

"It's not so bad." Greg stood over her shoulder, polishing his wrench.

Dani arched an eyebrow, standing over him with an elbow on her hip.

"Okay, it's…" Greg nodded out the window and continued in a whisper, "It's Mr. What's-His-Face and your brother. And it's better than it was."

Vic's face dropped when he walked through the door. Dani glared. What's-His-Face wrinkled his brow.

"Coffee, anyone?" Greg held the half-empty pot in his greasy mitt.

Mr. What's-His-Face's tone was slow, steady as he walked up to the car, running his finger along the striping. "That's not what I asked for." He took the cup Greg held out to him. One cream, two sugars.

Dani cringed, biting her lip as he looked the rest of the car over.

"Who did this?"

Dani raised her hand halfway.

"We all had something to do with it." Beads of sweat formed on Vic's temples. "We'll make it…"

"Even better." What's-His-Face sucked in his cheeks, nodding. "You took a chance and made it better than what I asked for. When can you take the '57s?"

Dani sat alone that night, clicking channels. Vic had told her not to wait up, but she wanted to catch the news. It still felt weird to watch it when she didn't have a school assignment requiring her to, but it was becoming routine. Even though she knew any really bad news would come by phone or a chaplain at the door, it helped her sleep better to know there wasn't anything new happening in Saudi Arabia and Kuwait, places she couldn't have located on a map last year.

Across town, Vic walked under the streetlights, pace brisk, hands in his pockets. Kari Andersen bounced beside him, perm bobbing as she double-timed to keep up.

Keep it to what I came here for. "I think it'll blow over and Dad'll be back home in a couple months. But she worries. That's just Dani."

Big green eyes gazed at him over blue plastic frames.

She'd be good looking if she'd tone down the Tammy Faye impression.

Vic chided himself. She wore too much paint for his taste, but it wasn't *that* extreme. And he knew Kari was just trying to do what she thought was right with Dani. He also knew he could smile and talk her into just about anything.

The pair halted in front of Dominic's Ristorante.

"Best Italian in town," Vic said. *Only Italian in town.*

Kari giggled, leaning in closer than he liked. "I can think of at least one I like better, *Signore* Grassigli."

He made himself look into her eyes. She was practically shaking, looking like she was trying to suppress that toothy smile of hers. He shrugged. "About Dani…"

The phone shook Dani awake. She wiped tears from her eyes, thankful the Marine Corps calling to let her know Daddy was dead was just a bad dream.

Shelly. Sobbing.

Between trying to shake the dream and the cobwebs, Dani didn't understand much of what Shelly said. Something about Bobby being mad.

Good. Maybe he'll get lost.

That Sunday, Dani strummed and sang harmony as Kari played the piano and sang:

My lips shall praise You
My Great Redeemer
My heart will worship
Almighty Savior

Dani had no idea why Kari had a change of heart, but she determined as she played that she wasn't going to put herself in that position again. Being part of the worship team meant too much to her.

After a couple times through the chorus, Dani stepped up to the microphone and put some rasp into her alto voice:

"You take my guilt away..."

Kari's back stiffened.

"Turn the darkest night to brightest day..."

Kari gave her a look over her glasses. *Fine.* Kari had told her a thousand times that it was okay to rock out a bit in youth group, but she needed to keep her vocals clean on Sunday mornings.

Probably not the best time to test my boundaries.

She fell back into clear-as-crystal harmony as Kari resumed the melody.

"You are the restorer of my soul..."

Kari stopped the song after a single time through, moving on to a pair of simple, traditional choruses, songs Dani figured their church had been singing since long before she was born.

Pastor Ian Stenger hobbled to the pulpit. After opening with a quick prayer, he continued, "Most of you know Victor Grassigli put his plans for a missions trip on hold. He would have left tomorrow morning, but he is staying here for now to keep his family business running. What you may not know is that he'll be doing some preaching here and in other churches around the area. I'd like to make sure we all keep him and his family in prayer as they navigate a difficult season."

Chapter Three

"Shelly talk to you?"

Dani looked up from what passed for a salad in Rio Flaco High's cafeteria to see Inferno's bass player. Up close, he looked a lot like the singer.

"Not since Friday." She wasn't at church. Hadn't answered the phone. Wasn't in Art class this morning.

"Guess I'll have to then," he said.

"Bell's any minute."

"I'll talk fast."

"Can bass players do anything fast?"

The bell rang. He snatched her books. "Thompson's English, right? C-wing?"

Dani suppressed a smile. "Don't you have your own class?"

"When's the last time you saw a bass player come in on time, anyway?"

She had to give him credit. In the two minutes it took to get to room C-17, he got out all he had to say. Bobby hurt his hand and was out for a couple weeks. Would she sit in on Inferno's gig next Friday? She reached out her hands as they reached the doorway.

"So you'll play?"

"I don't even know your name."

"I'm hurt."

"Well, Hurt," Dani lowered her voice, "I don't think my dad would like that."

"Wasn't asking him," he called after her as she slipped in the classroom, and the tardy bell rang.

L ate that afternoon, Dani leaned against the tool cabinet and looked on as Greg pulled the 426 Hemi from the Superbird.

"Your brother's good at making promises."

"Since when did you complain about overtime?"

Greg shrugged.

"Got plans? A girl?"

"Not the right time for that." A tint came over Greg's face. "Got my eyes on one, but…"

A buzz announced the door's opening.

"We're closed," Greg called over his shoulder.

Shelly hunkered into her stonewashed jean jacket in the open doorway.

"What happened to your eye?" Dani walked over to get a closer look.

"You know me, I'm a klutz," Shelly said, pulling away and teasing a strand of hair over the purplish bruise. "You give Cal an answer yet?"

"Who?"

"Bobby's bass player."

"There's no way Vic'll let me play at a bar."

"Who's telling?"

"Not hearing this." Greg put his hands to his ears and headed to the office. "Plausible deniability."

Dani could feel her pulse race. "Vic can't find out we were at that party. I'd be dead. And if Kari ever found out…"

"C'mon, Dani, it's just one show."

"If Daddy finds out I'm hanging out with that crowd, I'll get a one-way ticket to my grandparents' farm. In Iowa."

"Bobby's hurt, and they need someone who can play."

They needed someone who could play anyway.

"Why me? Wasn't Bobby mad last time?"

"He's afraid the band will kick him out if anyone else fills in. Says there's no way they'd make you permanent."

"Kari would kick me off the praise band if she knew we were even *listening* to the stuff they play."

"This is a big deal. There's gonna be some big shot promoter there." Shelly flashed a conspiratorial smile. "Little birdie told me Jon's got the hots for you."

"Who?"

Two days later, on Wednesday night, Dani packed up her hot pink Fender Strat—last year's Christmas present—and slipped a Petra cassette into the car stereo, cranking the dial as she headed out. By the time she reached Shelly's house, her friend was already coming out the door. Her eye looked better.

Amazing what a little makeup will do.

"Have fun at youth group," Shelly's mom called from the doorway.

"Sometimes I feel a hesitation—is it me or is it you?"

Shelly giggled as she slammed the GTO's door. Dani forced a smile.

"I only need some kind of clue—I just need an indication…"

"Ugh! Is that all you have?" Shelly popped the cassette out, fiddling with the radio dial. "You might as well have kept the 8-track player in this bucket."

"I never get away with anything," Dani said, squealing the tires.

"Maybe tonight's your night." Shelly pulled a fifth of something clear from her jacket pocket, shaking it.

Brakes.

"You promised you'd stop."

"We're not even to the corner yet. My mom's gonna see."

Dani feathered the gas. "I don't need this." She popped the cassette back in as she pulled to the intersection.

> *"It's not hard to miss a turn along the way...*
> *I know I've missed some in my day...*
> *And now I'm at another crossroad..."*

Dani bit her lip and turned the wheel right, toward the church.

"C'mon, you promised you'd play. And this," Shelly said, putting the bottle back in her jacket pocket, "is for Bobby. I won't even have any."

> *"And I don't know which way to go...*
> *My steps are ordered, and I know I'll find the way..."*

Dani gave her the eye as she hit the gas.

> *"When Your Word lights my path and I..."*

Shelly turned the stereo off. "We're gonna be late."

"Youth group starts at seven. We've got plenty of time. What you want to bet Kari talks about the dangers of liquor and rock 'n roll?"

Shelly looked around, pouting. The coast clear, she tossed the bottle out the window. "Happy?"

"Still shouldn't be doing this." Dani pulled a U-turn and gunned it.

𝔉ifteen minutes later, Dani pulled into the same house where they'd had the party last week—the drummer's house, she'd since learned. No one was there but Bobby, sitting on the stage trying to light one cigarette off another with his wrapped hand.

He tossed Dani a cassette and a crumpled piece of paper. "Setlist. Think you can play 'em?"

Dani gave it the once-over, jingling her keys. "Legs" by ZZ Top, "Panama" and "Runnin' with the Devil" by Van Halen, a couple of Mötley songs, Cinderella, Poison, an older one by The Knack. A half dozen titles she didn't recognize, probably Inferno's originals. None of it was allowed in her house.

"Looks simple enough."

"Guys will be here in a few minutes." Bobby headed out the door. "Don't hurt yourself trying to nail my solos."

Shelly smiled at Dani. "Your keys?"

"Not part of the deal."

The door slammed.

"Look, Bobby only agreed to let you sit in so we could have some time alone," Shelly said as the GTO horn blared.

"Thought it was because he hurt his hand. Nailing his solo." Dani unpacked her guitar case, tossing her keys down. "I'm only here for you."

"And Jon?" Shelly nudged her.

"Maybe a little, but…"

"C'mon, me and Bobby really need to talk."

"Cars-Are-For-Dri-Ving," Dani sang out as she checked her tuning. She adjusted the A-string. "Ving… ving."

"Alone," Shelly said, reaching for the case. "Away from the band and Marc's parents."

Dani shielded the keys.

Shelly sighed. "C'mon, you know we've been having problems."

"You've been going out three weeks."

Crocodile tears.

"Don't let him smoke in my car." *Vic's going to kill me if he finds out.*

Vic sat in the parking lot of Stony Creek First Church. He figured it would be another fifteen or twenty minutes before the pastor arrived, and the service wouldn't start for another forty minutes after that. He spread his notes on the dash. Not that he needed them. The sermon was rote by now. He tried to pray for the upcoming service and for the people of Stony Creek, to whom he would be preaching soon, but his mind wandered elsewhere.

"Help me have patience with her." As he always did when he was alone, he prayed more with his hands than his mouth. "I can't be Dad. I don't want to be Dad. I just want to get through this."

He closed his eyes and let his prayers wander. Dad's safety. Dani's. Wisdom to run the shop and make his father proud. For people to show up to hear him tonight. That he would preach well. That God would open the doors for him to get on the mission field soon.

He opened his eyes to tapping on the windshield. Pastor Logan, looking at his watch. The parking lot was full. He checked his own watch as he stepped out of the car. *Service starts in ten minutes.* He hated being late. And ten minutes early was late. He apologized.

The pastor laughed. "Looked like you were having revival all by yourself. Figured I'd let you know it's time to come share the wealth."

A hulking parishioner wearing a deputy sheriff's uniform stopped by the pair. "Nice car."

"Work in progress," Vic said, looking over the rusty '57 Chevy. "But it will be when we're done."

𝔄 n hour, two hymns, and three points later, Vic looked over the congregation. They were a quiet bunch, hard to read. *Wonder how much they've heard.*

"That brings us to the question. Are we our brother's keepers? Do we, like Cain, despise others because they're doing right when we know that we're not? Even if they're doing wrong, do we cast our brother aside? Or do we love one another? Do we protect one another, even when that means protecting someone from themselves? When we see our brothers doing something they shouldn't, do we restore them in love? Do we remember we could just as easily be the one who has fallen?" Vic set his weathered Bible on the pulpit as the organist began to play and congregants made their way to the altars.

After the service, Pastor Logan clapped him on the back. "I've never seen these folks so responsive. Let's schedule you again sometime this summer. You have a real gift. What's keeping you from the mission field you're so passionate about?"

"Dad got called to active duty, and someone needs to run the business. After he gets back, he'll retire from the Marines and, between him and my sister, they won't need me. Dani's more into that than I am, anyway. And better at it."

"Why not let her run it now?"

"After she graduates, maybe," Vic said. "Even then, I don't know if she could handle the business side of it. So, until then, I'll take care of my little sister and settle for preaching here and there when God opens the doors."

𝔇 ani fumbled with her gear as the butterflies in her stomach shifted into fourth and floored it. Jon had barely taken his eyes off her the whole rehearsal. Now, they were alone. She looked at her watch. *Shelly's got twenty minutes, or we'll never beat Vic home.* Wrapping up the last of the cords, she allowed herself a glance.

Jon leaned against the amps, eyeing her, sporting a devil-may-care grin.

A real rock star in the rough. "Won't miss Bobby as much as I thought."

Dani caught herself biting her lip again. She couldn't imagine they'd miss Bobby, the obvious weak link in the group, at all. She'd picked up the original songs quickly. Nothing all that complicated. Lots of flash, no real feel. She'd put her own stink on it and knew she'd blown Bobby out of the water.

"I'm dead if word gets around."

His look begged the question.

"My family wouldn't approve of me playing this kind of music. And my church definitely wouldn't."

Jon stepped closer. "If anyone from your church is at our show, it's not like they're going to admit it."

"I never get away with anything." Biting the lip again. *Stop that. It makes you look, like, five.* She glanced out the window. Still no Shelly.

"Relax." He put his hand on her back. Smirked.

Dani tensed. She met his gaze for a fraction of a second, felt blood rushing to her face.

"Not like you're a kid."

"For two more months, I am. Till April first."

Jon laughed. "No kidding? April Fool's Day?"

Wow, he's close. And a little sweaty.

"Mother's little fools," she said. "Me and my brother both. Six years apart, and she still couldn't hit a different day."

The thought of Mom hit her hard. *Don't start crying.*

Jon leaned in closer, cupped her chin.

I love you, Mom, but I can't think about you right now.

She'd never been kissed. If it was going to happen, she didn't want to be thinking about Mom, of all things.

Throttling engine. Tires throwing gravel. Her GTO's horn.

She pulled away.

He frowned. "Can't you stay a few more minutes?"

Wish I could. And I don't. Can I? Don't know. She checked her watch. "Gonna have to floor it to beat my brother home as it is."

"What's he gonna do?"

"If he knew I was here? You don't want to know," she said over her shoulder as she pulled her guitar case through the door. "*I* don't want to know."

Turning into the cold wind, she stopped in her tracks.

No Shelly. No Bobby.

Vic.

Chapter Four

Dani had never seen Vic's face that shade. She set her guitar next to Bobby's LA Kings jersey and blue jeans, folded neatly on the back seat.

Let him have the first word.

Vic stared straight ahead, jaw clenched, knuckles white on the steering wheel. He drove deliberately, shifts smooth, eyes on road, needle kissing fifty-five.

He never did know how to drive a muscle car.

"Say something." Dani tried not to fidget.

Fifteen minutes passed, the throaty growl of her GTO's 389 the only sound.

"Wasn't my idea," Dani said.

She thought she detected an eyebrow flicker, the jaw slacken.

"Won't do it again."

Vic exhaled sharply as he turned into the driveway. "Those guys are bad news."

"We were just playing music."

"What kind?"

Dani knew better than to answer.

Vic clenched his teeth. "No more hanging out with Shelly."

"She's my only friend. You can't tell me who to be friends with."

"Out of my hands." Vic sighed. "Her mom says you're a bad influence."

Dani followed him into the house. "I gotta straighten this out. Give me my keys."

Vic flashed his are-you-kidding-me stare.

"You can't take my car."

"You're grounded."

"Quit playing Dad." Dani slumped her shoulders. "How am I supposed to get to school?"

Vic shoved the keys in his pocket. "That big yellow thing that drives by every morning…"

Dani stifled a groan.

"You can have them back when Dad says you can."

"You're not really going to tell him?"

"No." Vic cocked his head, locking eyes. "You are."

Ring.

"Perfect timing."

Vic's face fell when he answered. Dani could make out Kari's muffled voice.

"I already know." Vic rolled his eyes. "I'll handle…"

A flurry of jabbering interrupted him.

"What station?"

Dani heard the reply clearly: "Any!"

President Bush seemed to look straight at Dani as Vic backed away from the TV.

"Tonight, the battle has been joined," the president intoned.

"What's happening?" Dani said.

Vic turned the volume up.

"This military action, taken in accord with United Nations resolutions and with the consent of the United States Congress, follows months of constant and virtually endless diplomatic activity on the part of the United Nations, the United States, and many, many other countries."

"Did they start fighting? Is Dad near…"

"Be quiet, or neither of us will know."

"…this past weekend, in a last-ditch effort, the Secretary-General of the United Nations went to the Middle East with peace in his heart—his second such mission. And he came back from Baghdad with no progress at all in getting Saddam Hussein to withdraw from Kuwait. Now, the twenty-eight countries with forces in the Gulf area have exhausted all reasonable efforts to reach a peaceful solution and have no choice but to drive Saddam from Kuwait by force."

Dani shut her eyes, emitting a slight whimper as she prayed, "Please bring Daddy home."

"Arab leaders sought what became known as an Arab solution," the president continued, "only to conclude that Saddam Hussein was unwilling to leave Kuwait."

When she opened her eyes, Vic sat cross-legged in front of the screen.

"I didn't think they'd have to fight," he said. "Dad could be gone a long time. Maybe years."

Dani stifled a sob.

"As I report to you, air attacks are underway against military targets in Iraq."

The president seemed so nonchalant. Deadpan.

He doesn't know our dad's there.

"We are determined to knock out Saddam Hussein's nuclear bomb potential. We will also destroy his chemical weapons facilities. Much of Saddam's artillery and tanks will be destroyed."

Dani took little comfort in the president's promise that all possible steps were being taken to ensure the safety of Americans and their allies. The president made it clear he had no intention to remove American troops until Iraqi forces were out of Kuwait.

"Why now?" Dani said. Vic didn't seem to hear the question.

"Some may ask: Why act now?" President Bush said. "Why not wait? The answer is clear: The world could wait no longer. Sanctions, though having some effect, showed no signs of accomplishing their objective..."

The rest of the president's speech droned on, and Dani zoned out until he circled back to talk of possible chemical and nuclear weapons in the enemy's arsenal.

"You don't think they'd use..."

"No." Vic's voice was firm, but his face told a different story.

"While the world waited, Saddam Hussein met every overture of peace with open contempt. While the world prayed for peace, Saddam prepared for war..."

"Do you think Daddy's going to be gone for my graduation?"

"I've told the American people before that this will not be another Vietnam," the president said. "And I repeat that here tonight. Our troops will have the best possible support in the entire world, and they will not be asked to fight with one hand tied behind their back. I'm hopeful that this fighting will not go on for long and that the casualties will be held to an absolute minimum. No president can easily commit our sons and daughters to war..."

What about our daddies?

"They are our nation's finest. Ours is an all-volunteer force, magnificently trained, highly motivated. The troops know why they're there. Tonight, America and the world are deeply grateful to them and to their families. And let me say to everyone listening or watching tonight: When the troops we've sent in finish their work, I am determined to bring them home as soon as possible. Tonight, as our forces fight, they and their families are in our prayers..."

Vic and Dani sat in silence as the president asked God to bless America, and the station switched to an endless stream of pundits discussing what they'd just heard.

Chapter Five

The next morning, Dani tried not to pout as she navigated through sophomores, freshmen, and middle school kids to take a seat near the back of the bus.

Bet I'm the only senior. Probably the only person over sixteen.

The route differed from her ten-minute drive to school. She couldn't imagine a longer way to get from point A to point B. And it was loud. Feeling a headache coming on, she slipped on Walkman headphones and cranked the volume.

Someone tapped her on the shoulder. Stoner. *Okay, so there's at least one other senior.*

"See your dad didn't kill you," he said as she lifted an earphone.

"He's busy fighting the war."

She tried to ignore him. He didn't seem to notice.

"Grass, right? How'd you get in Inferno if you don't smoke weed?"

"Grassigli. And I'm not in Inferno, Stoner." *Don't call names. You're better than that.*

"They usually just let chicks shake a tambourine or something." Stoner laughed long, stopping abruptly as if he'd forgotten what was funny. "Show sucked till you got there."

Dani looked around for another open seat. Nada.

"It true? Y'know?" He snickered. "You and Jon Ryder?"

Dani felt her cheeks tingle.

"We played."

Another snicker.

"Music. And just twice."

"Not what I heard."

Dani started down the aisle as the bus turned the corner and the school came into view.

"Stay seated until the bus comes to a complete stop!"

Dani retreated. Did the driver have to yell?

"What's your hurry?" Stoner slid over to make room for her.

Dani sat in her own seat and turned toward the window.

"See you at the next show?"

As soon as the driver braked, Dani hit the aisle, first out the door, and ran straight into Shelly. Arms folded. Waiting. Scowling. Makeup heavier than normal.

The rest of the week dragged by. No call from Daddy. Dani thought of him night and day, praying he was safe. Most of the news about the war showed American jets blowing the Iraqi army to bits, but she knew war was, as Daddy put it, "a dangerous game of subtraction." The Trans Am parked in the garage was an ever-present reminder that some don't come back.

To make matters worse, all efforts to reason with Vic about her car fell on deaf ears. She'd have to wait for Daddy's phone call. Knowing she'd have to bring that up when he was finally able to call killed her. Nothing in this world ate her insides like the sound of Daddy's voice when he was disappointed in her.

She felt wrong about the whole plan Shelly had cooked up. Vic may be a pain, but he had put a lot on hold so she could stay in Rio Flaco to finish her senior year. Otherwise, it would have been off to their grandparents' farm in Iowa, where she had no friends.

Dani put that out of her mind, half hoping Daddy wouldn't call too soon. It would only make it harder for her to do what she had to do this Friday. Shelly was counting on her.

Greg ran his hands along the lines of the '57 Chevys, prattling on about the work Dani had done on them. Vic couldn't disagree. Mr. Wilkins had given them free rein on the paint and design, asking only that the interior be kept as close to original as possible.

Dani ran wild with one—yellow flames spilling over the hood and side panels, fading into orange as they licked the fins, all overlaying a custom deep ocean-blue, just a shade lighter than the classic Harbor Blue. The other was Matador Red and India Ivory. Safer. Classic. Pristine. A real textbook restoration.

"Parts should be in Monday," Greg said. "Gimme a day or two, barring disaster, and they'll purr like kittens."

"Ahead of schedule for a change," Vic said, his mind elsewhere. He buried himself in paperwork as Greg got back to work.

Should probably call Shelly's mother. Maybe she's cooled off by now. Then again, maybe she was right. It occurred to him for the first time Dani could be the ringleader. Either way, Dani didn't make friends easily. Neither of them did. *Hard to make lasting friendships when you move all the time.*

He buried his head in his hands. "The last thing in the world I want is to send her away."

Greg chuckled. Vic wondered how long he'd been standing in the doorway.

"As if you could run this shop without her."

Vic looked out the window. Was that snow? It had been cold lately. Record lows, he'd heard. But this was still California. He hadn't seen snow since the family moved out here. He thought how cold it had been all week and had a fleeting moment of guilt about leaving Bobby on the side of the road. *Probably should have left him his shirt.*

"I definitely can't do the detail work." Greg seemed eager to change the subject. "And we've seen your handiwork. Face it, until Gunny gets back…"

Vic massaged his wrist, making a fist and loosening it. It still hurt from tossing Bobby out of Dani's car. "Some things are more important than the shop. Besides, we won't have to wait long. Saddam's crazy if he doesn't surrender before we're doing anything that puts Dad in danger."

"You do know what he does, right? I mean, I know he doesn't tell Dani, but…" Greg seemed to think better of saying more.

"He fixes Jeeps."

"Humvees nowadays, but where exactly do you think Jeeps break down during a war, Skippy?" Greg sat opposite the desk. "Anyway, you want me to run those guys off?"

Limp or no limp, Vic knew Greg could make good on his offer. But what did he know about the guys Dani hung out with?

Greg locked eyes. "Got my kid with me this weekend, but just say the word, Brother. I'll go have a talk with 'em Monday. They'll stay away."

Vic fingered his mother's Bible on the desk corner, right where Dad had set it five years ago. He knew if he opened to the ribbon bookmark, it would take him to the Sermon on the Mount. "Blessed are the peacemakers" and all that. He let his gaze fall on the family pictures taped to the window. Dani, a toddler then, in Sergeant Grassigli's arms, her head buried in his shoulder. It was the day Dad got his third stripe.

"What would Gunny do?" Vic said, returning Greg's stare.

"What do I need this for?" Dani repeated, looking over both sides of the fake ID.

"You said you'd play the show," Shelly said.

"Not if it's someplace I'm gonna need that. Playing that kind of music's bad enough. You know I promised my parents I'd only play godly music when they got me my guitar."

Shelly tucked the ID into Dani's blouse pocket. "You've got to do this. Look, I can't be seen with you."

"Afraid you'll be influenced?"

Shelly rolled her eyes and headed to class, Dani on her heels.

"C'mon, Shel."

"They can't cancel this show," Shelly said as they approached her class. "It means everything to Bobby."

"They can find someone else."

"By tonight?"

"I'm grounded."

"No kidding. At least you're not grounded from your boyfriend."

"How am I supposed to get there without my car?"

"This is Vic we're talking about." Shelly smirked. "The keys…"

"… are in the cookie jar," they said together, giggling.

"And we both know he'll be asleep by ten," Shelly said.

"I'll try, but if I get caught, I might as well join a convent." *A convent in Iowa. Wonder what that even looks like. Sacred Sisters of the Corn.*

"Pick me up around the block quarter after ten. Show starts at eleven." Shelly slipped into the classroom under her teacher's disapproving look as the bell rang.

Great. Third tardy. One more thing for Vic to read about.

Ed Wilkins fingered the steering wheel in the blue Chevy, leaning out the window. "How's your dad?"

"Good as can be in a war zone." Vic didn't want to think about it.

"Left the business in good hands," Wilkins said, admiring the detailing.

"I'll tell Dani when she's home from school. Make her day."

"Say, hop in. Let's go to your place."

Vic couldn't imagine what for, but if the shop's best customer wanted to visit the house, he wasn't going to argue. He just hoped Dani hadn't left a mess in the kitchen.

As soon as Wilkins turned into the driveway, he insisted, "Show me the T.A."

Nothing too unusual about that. Dad showed off his car once in a while.

Wilkins took a few seconds to compliment Dani's GTO before turning his attention to the Pontiac. He took his time, examining every inch. Sat in the driver's seat. Sat in the passenger seat. Fiddled with the radio dial. Popped the hood.

"You the man in charge now?"

Vic saluted. "Sergeant's orders."

Wilkins ran his finger along the blue racing stripe down to the air intake on the Firebird's hood. "Gotta have it. Name your price."

"Mr. Wilkins, I don't think you understand."

"Half a million."

"Dad's turned that down before."

"Give me a number." Wilkins flourished his checkbook.

"Might as well ask Dad to sell Dani."

"Thought you were in charge?"

Vic recounted the car's story.

"Maybe just a drive?"

"I'm sorry, Mr. Wilkins, but it only comes out for shows. And only Dad drives it. Ever. Written in stone. Wish I could."

Mr. Wilkins studied him. "Sell me the GOAT, then."

Chapter Six

Only Teddy Bear was home when Dani arrived. Good. Facing Vic would just make it harder. The dog ambled behind into her room.

She opened her curtain enough to see the driveway before running through the setlist again. She was sure Vic wouldn't even recognize the newer songs. She could just tell him they were Stryper tunes. But the older ones, from before the family came to Christ? The last thing she needed was Vic hearing "Runnin' with the Devil" coming from her room. *If he ever found my cassette case, he'd have kittens.*

Two times through and she had all the cover songs down.

Learning Bobby's parts on Inferno's originals took longer. *Overplay much?* "Seriously, you don't have to fill every hole. Oh, well, at least the lyrics stink." She mumbled them, trying to learn them as she played:

> *I got my mind in the gutter*
> *Got my mind in the gutter*
> *Got my mind in the gutter*
> *And my body ain't far behind*

Teddy Bear whined and hid in the closet.

"I'm with you. Who writes this stuff?"

Three hours later, Vic still hadn't come home. *Wonder if he got stuck at the shop?* Could be he was going to pick up the next project for Mr. Wilkins. She decided not to worry about it. Turning the volume on her clock radio loud enough to rouse her without waking Vic and checking to make sure it was on a Christian station just in case he did hear, she set the alarm for nine-thirty. It was going to be a late night.

"Got myself in this situation
I'm not so sure about..."

Dani slapped at the snooze button. "Shut up, Amy."
As the clock hit the floor, the Dove award-winner kept going.

"Climbing in where there's temptation
Can I get back out?"

Dani felt through the dark for the clock. By the time she held it up by its cord, Amy Grant was belting the chorus.

"Better wise up
Better think twice
Never leave room for compromise
You better wise up
Better get smart
And use your head to guard your heart..."

Dani finished the chorus for her as she yanked the cord out of the wall.
"It's gonna get rough, so you better wise up."
"Better get my thoughts together before they come undone," she muttered.
She heard Vic snoring in the living room. *Must have had a long day. Vic never sleeps on the couch. Good thing he sleeps like a box of rocks.* She peeked in on him. He hadn't changed out of his coveralls, the top splotched with grease. *He wouldn't allow me on the furniture like that.*
Teddy Bear nuzzled against Dani's leg, erupting in a yawn.
"Shhh, go lie down."

Dani used a washcloth to muffle the sound as she picked the keys out of the cookie jar. So far, so good. She couldn't stop the door to the garage from creaking a little, but she was sure that wouldn't stir her brother. She'd seen him sleep through hurricanes when the family was stationed on the East Coast. She backed out quietly, making sure the door didn't slam as she stepped into the garage and turned the light on.

Nothing in the garage but Daddy's Trans Am.

"Where's my car?!" Dani clapped her hand over her mouth as the blood rushed to her face. *Who does he think he is?* Her hands twitched as she balled her fists. She wanted to scream. *How dare he move my car?*

She stepped back inside, huffing, puffing, and ready to pound him. *Think, Dani, think. You don't want to punch a one-way ticket to the farm. But if I don't get to the show, Shelly will never forgive me. I promised.*

She crept into Daddy's room, feeling around on his dresser. In the darkness, her forearm brushed against cold metal. She was sure it was the frame from her favorite picture of Mom in her pure-white wedding dress. Careful not to knock it over, she reached behind and retrieved Daddy's spare Trans Am keys from Mom's old jewelry box.

Shelly directed Dani to park next to Bobby's rusted-out junker outside On the Rocks Bar.

"Ain't exactly Sunset Strip," Dani said as she parked Daddy's Trans Am.

A gorilla in leather stood between the girls and the entrance.

"We're with the band," Shelly said, pointing at Dani's guitar case.

"Didn't book Kids Incorporated," Gorilla said.

Dani fished through her pockets for her fake ID as Shelly handed hers to the bouncer and smiled sweetly.

"Yeah, whatever," he said, nodding her in. "But not you. No, ID, no entry."

"I promise I had it," Dani said, drawing an exaggerated eye roll from Shelly.

Thirty seconds later, Shelly came back with Cal.

"Don't care," Gorilla said before he could speak. "No ID, no entry."

Cal shoved a crumpled green wad into the giant's mitts.

Gorilla took a minute to count it before he stood aside. "Happy twenty-first, Toots."

Smoke stung Dani's eyes as she stepped in and tried to adjust to the dim light.

"C'mon, we're on in fifteen minutes," Cal said. "Was beginning to wonder if you'd show."

"Beginning to wish I hadn't," Dani said as a drunk wolf-whistled from the other end of the room. *Lord, please don't let Daddy's car get scratched.*

Dani tuned up and went to look for the rest of the band. She found them outside the back door, smoking and joking. They must not have seen her.

"We all agreed, no fooling around with the help." First time she'd heard the drummer—Marc something-or-other—string more than three words together.

Cal was the only one that didn't laugh.

"Nothing happened." Jon said, coughing.

"Find yourself a by-the-hour place after the show and have fun." She couldn't see Bobby around the corner, but she knew his voice. "She's a rental anyway."

Dani's neck stiffened. She balled her fists and started toward them.

"Don't talk about her like that," Cal and Jon said, almost in unison.

❝Just play 'em like I wrote 'em." Bobby leaned against the Peavey amps as Inferno sound checked. "If you can."

Dani turned her back to him. *View's better the other direction, anyway.* Marc sat, twirling his sticks and pounding rudiments against his jeans. Having finished her sound check five minutes ago, Dani could relate. She stole a glance at Jon, leaning against the bar chatting with the bartender. If he noticed, he didn't let on.

She knew nobody she knew would come to this kind of place, but she scanned the crowd every few minutes, just in case. *What would I do if I saw a familiar face anyway? Hide behind the amps? Sneak out the back door? Shelly would kill me.*

She put the thoughts behind her as Jon jumped on the stage, grabbed the mic and shouted something unintelligible to the crowd as the band launched into Cinderella's "Gypsy Road."

After the first song, Bobby skulked off, stopping to say a few words to some old guy on his way to Shelly's table. *Is that the same creep from the party?* He sure stared at her the same way, nodding dismissively at Bobby. She did her best to focus on the song.

By the third song, Dani lost herself in the performance. The crowd was easily twice as big as any she'd played in front of before and more kept coming. She thought she saw a fight break out. Hard to tell through the layers of smoke and the cheap strobe lights. Whatever it was settled quickly.

The set went smoothly until Jon announced the first of Inferno's originals. *Great, the ooh, aah, baby song. My favorite.* She played the intro note-for-note like she'd heard it on the demo tape, letting the song build through the first bridge and chorus. *Solo time. How mad can he be if I improve it a little?* Dani smiled, pointing out into the haze in the general direction of Bobby and Shelly's table as she dove in. *Needs something a little more Stevie Ray-esque.* She played fewer than half the notes Bobby crammed into the eight-bar solo, but that didn't stop the crowd from jumping to their feet by the time she hit the key change into the final chorus.

As the show continued, mugs of beer and shot glasses of something clear starting piling up on Dani's amp. When Inferno finally took five, she caught the waitress bringing another and tried to wave her off.

"I don't drink."

"Don't care if you flush 'em." The bags under her eyes had bags. "They keep buying 'em, I keep bringing 'em."

"It's how they pay us," Jon chimed in, helping himself to a glass for each hand and stashing the others behind the amps.

"What was that?!" Bobby stood at the edge of the stage.

"I'm just a rental. You can play however you want to next show."

Before he could argue the point, Inferno kicked into its second set. The band locked in with Dani as she let loose, playing the songs the way she thought they should be played.

Jon hit the growing stash behind the amp from time to time, sometimes downing them himself, other times taking one back for Marc. If it affected his voice, Dani couldn't tell. As the night wore on, Cal became more animated in his motions. Probably for the drummer's benefit. *He's dragging a little, but at least he's keeping Marc from playing like a runaway train.*

During the second set of Inferno originals, Bobby emerged red-faced through the smoke. She played a few bars exactly like Bobby had on the tape until he eased up and turned around. Stepping away from the mic, she shouted, "Don't want you thinking I couldn't if I wanted to!" and switched back to her own rendition.

He flipped a lewd gesture over his shoulder.

Who cares? Shelly can do better anyway.

Three more songs, an overly dramatized exit, and an encore later, Inferno was wrapping up.

"Got my mind in the gutter…"

Jon stifled a cough.

"Mind in the gutter…"

Cough. Cough.

"I got my mind in the gutt—"

Jon stepped away from his mic in a coughing fit.

Throwing a quick glance at Cal—nowhere near a mic—Dani stepped up to Jon's mic and belted:

"And my body ain't far behind."

Pandemonium broke out in the bar as she leaned into the rest of the chorus.

"Got my mind in the gutter,
Mind in the gutter,
Come on down
And get a little dirty with me."

Dani wasted no time packing after the show. Her little stunt at the end felt like the right thing to do at the time, but the crowd's response made her skin crawl. *Why did it have to be that song?* By far Inferno's worst, she hated it more with every catcall and lewd compliment the men in the crowd hurled her way.

Now all she wanted was to get away from here, but Shelly was nowhere to be found. *Typical.*

Outside, Jon leaned against a new Fiero, swigging a Corona and talking with Paunchy Mullet. *How many has he had? Nine, at least.*

Jon called her over. "Want you to meet our promoter."

"Tom Basil."

Dani liked Paunchy Mullet better. His leer reminded her of Teddy Bear's every time Daddy fired up the grill.

"Dani Grass, eh?" Mr. Basil said.

"Grassigli."

"Not no more. Grass is better." Easily in his thirties, Mr. Basil made no attempt at subtlety as he sized her up. "This, I can sell."

"This ain't for sale." Dani headed toward the Trans Am to load her gear, keeping an eye out for Shelly. Bobby's junker was gone.

Jon was still talking to the promoter after she'd finished loading.

"Business is business," Basil said.

Dani considered lighting out but couldn't bring herself to. Fastening the top button on her blouse, she approached as Jon slurred, "But he's my best friend."

Basil shrugged. "Bobby couldn't carry her gear."

"Wouldn't want him to," Dani said. "But is Shelly with him?"

"Last I saw." Jon threw the empty bottle against the back wall and slid into his car.

"You're not driving?"

"What're you, my mother?" Jon sported a sloppy grin.

She looked over at Mr. Basil. "C'mon, you can't let him…"

"Not going my way." Basil nodded toward a black Cadillac. "Give you a lift if you want one, though."

Dani turned her back to the older man, exhaling sharply. She knew she shouldn't be alone with Jon, especially when he was three sheets to the wind. She knew Vic wouldn't approve. Daddy would blow a gasket. Kari would kick her off the praise team for good this time if she found out. *But he's not going to call a cab.* She motioned toward Daddy's car. "Hop in."

The sun peeked over the horizon as Dani pulled into the garage. She wasn't sure whether the tingling she felt down to her toes was fear that Vic might be up or the lingering effects of her first kiss.

She hadn't intended to let it get as far as it did, but she'd had no idea how hard his life was. *Imagine being thrown out on the streets like that by your own parents.* And he said he'd never seen anyone so pretty. Daddy was the only one who'd ever said anything like that to her. *Maybe it was the booze talking.* It still felt good. He said he'd always wanted a girl like her, a girl who didn't give it up easy. She felt a flush rise to her cheeks. *At least I didn't go into his trailer.* She couldn't deny part of her wanted to when he asked. *Wonder if he'll call.* She caught herself making that silly lip-biting grin again.

He hadn't made it easy to say good night.

Careful to close the car door quietly, Dani straightened her blouse and soft-pedaled into the house.

Vic. Head in hands. Sobbing.

Vic never cries.

She'd prepared her defense the whole drive home, just in case he was up. Don't answer any questions. Change the focus by yelling about her car being taken away. Start an argument about something else. If all else fails, cry about missing Daddy.

She hung her head.

"I'm sorry."

He just sat there, shaking.

Dani bit her lip, fought back tears. "I said I'm sorry. I won't do it again."

Nothing. Dani sat opposite him, reached for his hand.

"I've been nothing but trouble."

Sweet Trouble. That's what Mom had always called her. *Nothing sweet about this, though. Vic's been nothing but good to me.* She could feel mascara running down her face as she stopped trying to stem the tears.

A full five minutes later, Vic lifted bleary eyes.

"It's Dad."

Chapter Seven

Two days later, Dani slumped in the pew beside Vic during evening service. They'd missed that morning, something they hadn't done in as long as Dani could remember. The singing, the sermon, all white noise. Dani's mind was elsewhere.

At some point, Pastor Stenger must have called them forward. She barely remembered walking to the front, Vic's hand under her elbow, as the pastor explained that a Humvee had fallen from a lift. Tony, as everyone at church knew him, had pushed two other mechanics out of harm's way, but the vehicle had crushed both his legs. He wouldn't be coming home for at least a couple months and, when he did, it was unlikely he would ever walk again.

Should probably close my eyes, Dani thought as the pastor started to pray. Shelly looked down every time Dani looked over at her. Everyone else's heads were bowed until they all said, "Amen."

After the service, well-wishers with questions she couldn't answer bombarded Dani from every side until Vic whisked her off to the truck. He talked as he drove, but he may as well have been talking into the air. He'd been talking nonstop since yesterday.

Just trying to get me out of my funk.

"What did you do with my car?" It was the first time she'd thought about it since she heard the news about Daddy and her voice came off sharper than she'd intended. She immediately felt dumb for asking.

Vic took his time before answering in a clipped tone. "It's at the shop. Broke down while I took Mr. Wilkins out for a ride."

"Without asking me?"

"He's our best customer."

At least he didn't sell it. Would've served me right. She hated to admit it, but he was being pretty cool. He hadn't even mentioned her taking Daddy's car or how late she'd been out Friday night. Of course, she hadn't volunteered that information, either. She half wished he'd ask.

"Going to take a while to get the parts," Vic said, matter-of-fact.

Dani shrugged and retreated into her funk.

"C'mon, get mad about it. Get something. I almost sold it. Mr. Wilkins took back his offer when it threw a rod."

Funk over. If he was looking for emotion, he'd found the right button to push.

"My car?"

"Title says Fidelis, sis."

She glared straight ahead. "Daddy gave that to me for my birthday."

"Your sixteenth. Nothing's really yours till your eighteenth."

Vic tried to catch her eye. *Does he have to be so smug?* He probably intended that as the opener for one of those brotherly lectures she loved so much. Probably Old Number 231: "Using Your Gifts Responsibly." Or maybe the one about how much she needed him to look out for her. *Not going to let him see me cry.* She stared at the stop sign as Vic coasted. The car was still rolling when she stepped out.

"Stay away from those guys, or I'll put it in the front yard with a cardboard sign," he called after her as she slammed her door. The rest of what he said was muffled, but she heard enough to know it was something about what Gunny would do.

Shivering, she headed toward home. Vic followed for a couple hundred yards, trying to get her back in the truck. He tried arguing, cajoling, demanding.

Narrowing her eyes, Dani stopped and looked straight at him. "I can handle myself."

He threw his hands in the air and floored it, leaving her to handle the five miles to home as she screamed words she'd never have used if he could hear her until the truck disappeared over the horizon. She looked up at the graying sky and the road ahead. *Wish I'd have worn flats.*

𝕍ic rubbed his temples as he rolled down the window. Flashing lights always triggered his migraines. He fished out his license and registration, shutting his eyes as he held them out the window.

"Any idea how fast you were driving?" A woman's voice.

Vic squinted. She wasn't much older than he. Kind of cute in the uniform, red hair pulled back tight under her cap. He shook his head. "Five, maybe seven miles an hour?"

"In a fifty." Her tone was business-like, monotone, but friendly enough. "No flashers. Having trouble with your truck?"

The lights reflecting off her badge and the mirrors made his head throb. He looked away, shutting his eyes and pointing down the road. "No, Officer. I was just following that girl there."

It sounded like the officer was trying not to let the hint of urgency creep into her voice as she spoke into her radio. "I've got a 10-44-60."

He heard a car door close somewhere behind him.

"I need you to look up at me, sir." Still business-like. Still monotone. Less friendly.

When he complied, he found himself staring into the business end of a Magnum flashlight.

"Any drugs? Weapons? Anything in the car we should be aware of?"

He flashed the best grin he could manage with his head threatening to explode. "Just a Bible."

"Sir, I'm going to need you to step out of the vehicle."

Humor's not her strong suit.

ani had three miles to go and heels in hand when the rain started. She knew she looked like a drowned rat when the Fiero pulled up beside her, and the tinted window slid down to reveal Jon grinning like the Cheshire Cat. He gave half a nod toward the passenger seat.

Like something straight off an MTV video.

She flopped in, laughing despite herself. The first time she'd laughed in days. "I must look terrible," she said, running her hands through her tangled hair.

He didn't deny it, but the way he looked at her made her feel light-headed. She caught herself biting her lip again as she felt color rise in her cheeks.

He wiped mascara off her cheek with his fingertips and took her hand in his over the gear shift.

Smooth shifts. He really knows how to drive a sports car. The needle pushed past sixty as they passed the speed limit sign.

"Can't drive fifty-five?"

He grinned, making no attempt to hide the fact that he was looking her up and down from the corner of his eye. Dani felt as if her whole body was going to contract. Or explode.

"You can't take me home," she said after they'd driven a few minutes in silence. *Vic would have a cow.*

"Wouldn't dream of it." The car drifted, spitting gravel as he leaned into her, driving with his legs.

She froze when he put his hand on her knee and pressed his lips to hers. She closed her eyes, praying he wasn't closing his as Winger's "She's Only Seventeen" blared through the speakers.

y the time Vic convinced the rookie cop he wasn't drunk, high, or stalking "with intent to place anyone in reasonable fear for his or her safety," as she put it, more than half an hour had passed. He fumed, remembering how amused the older cop seemed to be when his zealous partner—Deputy Julie Porter, according to her name tag—called the K9 unit. *Ah well, could have been worse if he hadn't recognized me from when I preached at his church. And I did end up getting to invite her to church.*

He turned the wipers on as the drizzle gave way to a steady shower. After an hour combing every side street he could imagine Dani might have taken, he decided she'd probably beat him home.

"Hope she got a ride," he said as thunder pealed.

He decided to check one more place before heading home, the only other place he could imagine her going. *Say what you will about Dani, she's a homebody at heart.* He'd told her not to go there, but that didn't seem to stop her from doing what she wanted lately. And Vic knew she wouldn't be content staying away long. Besides, it was on the way.

As soon as the door opened at Shelly's house, he knew he'd made a mistake. Dani wasn't there. Shelly wasn't, either.

"Thought I told you to keep Dani away from her." Ms. Emmett looked fit to be tied. "She never got into trouble before she started hanging out with your sister."

Vic knew better, but he wasn't interested in having that conversation while standing in the rain. Not until he knew Dani was home and dry, at least. He tried to break it off, but Ms. Emmett was determined to give him an earful.

"I found condoms in Shelly's dresser," she said. "Shelly swore they were a friend's and Shelly wouldn't lie to me. What other friend could they possibly belong to?"

Vic had a few ideas but thought better of saying them out loud.

"Do you have any idea how hard it is for a single mother trying to raise a daughter right?"

Vic was afraid if she got any louder, she'd attract the neighbors' attention, rain or no rain.

"Shelly doesn't need that kind of influence. And what kind of a Christian are you, anyway, letting your sister live like that? Aren't you afraid she's going to get a reputation?"

Twenty minutes later, soaked to the skin and having given up on getting a word in edgewise, Vic crawled back into the truck and laid his head on the steering wheel. "Father, I don't have what it takes to be Dad."

ani's head reeled and every fiber of her being tingled. Jon had kissed her most of the drive here. She was surprised he'd managed to keep his car on the road.

I shouldn't be here with him—not alone. What was it Kari said about girls and guys being alone? Dani glanced at the purity ring Kari handed out after that youth group meeting and tried to remember how she'd put it. She couldn't recall exactly, but she remembered the game they'd played to illustrate whatever the point was and how she and Shelly had giggled hysterically while trying to stuff toothpaste back into the tube. The whole youth group had gone home messy that night.

I'm not going to let it get too far. Just kissing, nothing else. She knew neither Kari nor Vic would approve of even that, to say nothing of Daddy, even if Jon did need this time alone with her. She was his safe haven. He kept saying so. No one, not even Daddy, had ever said anything like that to her before. She'd never felt so scared and excited at the same time, as if someone had sucked all the oxygen out of the world.

"Won't your brother come looking for you here?" Jon walked up behind her, putting his hands on her hips as Dani fumbled with the lock.

"We never work Sundays." Dani leaned back into him as she pushed the door, turning around to kiss him, suddenly not minding the rain. "We're safe."

Jon gawked like a kid in a candy store when Dani turned on the lights. "Like classics?" she said.

He ran his hand along the fins of a '61 Cadillac DeVille that must have come in over the weekend. "My dad had one like this when I was little," Jon said, his mood sobering.

He seemed to have a hard time talking about his parents, especially his dad. He had mentioned them kicking him out of the house six or seven times starting when he was fifteen—almost six years ago. By the time he was seventeen, he'd said, he just stayed gone.

"Hope it had a better paint job than this one," Dani said, holding his hand as she looked the car over, sizing up what needed to be done. Whoever owned it last apparently couldn't decide what color they wanted. At least it didn't have much rust, but the chrome would need to be completely redone.

"Blue," he said. He sounded blue all of a sudden.

Bet I can make him feel better. She gave him her best smile as he turned her around, picked her up, and set her on the edge of the Cadillac's long trunk. He looked past her, almost like he was sizing up the potential of laying down on the car. Dani sat up straight, looking into his eyes and hooking her thumbs in his belt loops. She twisted away when his hands started to explore, smiling when he moved them back to her shoulders and moved in, kissing her deeply. By the time his hands started roaming again, she was practically gasping for breath.

Is it really that big a deal as long as the clothes stay on?

Looking him directly in the eye, she took his hands in hers and redirected them safely to her waist. Holding out her hand, afraid she was chasing him away, she showed him the purity ring and explained what it stood for. "So, watch your hands, mister."

Vic had worried, prayed, cried, paced, stared outside into the thunderstorm, called the police, screamed, and worried some more. On top of that, it was almost three hours past time for him to be asleep. By the time he heard the back door creek, he was spoiling for a fight.

Dani looked like a deer in the headlights when he flipped on the light switch, her hair a tangled mess like it always used to be when they'd gone swimming as kids. Her blouse was crumpled, but wherever she'd been, she'd managed to drip dry.

"Button up. You look like a streetwalker." He shook his head. "Who were you with?"

Dani pulled the top of her blouse closed, biting her bottom lip like she always did when she was nervous. Vic almost smiled, remembering her making that same face when she was two years old. No time for that, Vic did his best to make his face look like Dad's when he was preparing a tongue-lashing. Teddy Bear ambled in from the living room and plopped between them, nuzzling Dani's hand.

"We were just talking." Her voice quavered, and she fidgeted with her feet. Mom and Dad always knew Dani was stretching the truth when she did that. Back then, the stories were harmless enough. Vic saw her stiffen, tears starting to well. "Oh my gosh, you don't believe me?"

Teddy Bear let out a half-hearted growl.

"No."

She groaned, storming to her room, her dog at her heels. "If I'm going to get blamed anyway, I might as well actually do something."

Vic shoved his foot into the doorway before Dani could slam it. *Bad idea.* He screamed.

Slamming the door open instead, Dani retreated to her bed, throwing herself on the pillows. "Go away."

"Love to. Not an option." *Not for a couple more months, anyway.*

ani sat in the school commons the next day, yawning and doodling on her book cover. Between the flowers and guitars she'd drawn, she'd tried out a dozen ways to sign *Dani Ryder. Dani Ryder. Danielle Ryder. Nah, Dani Ryder.*

She covered her handiwork when Cal approached, heat rising in her cheeks.

"So, you're playing with us again?" he said.

"News to me."

"It's all Jon's talked about."

"Funny, we've talked about everything but." *Like how much he loves his little brother even though Mom always favored him. And how fine he thinks I am.* She caught herself smiling and looked away.

"Maybe he's waiting till Bobby cools down," Cal said.

Dani suppressed a scowl at the mention of that name.

"He wasn't happy about being demoted to rhythm guitar, but Basil insisted."

Another name she could do without hearing again.

"Listen, sooner or later, he's going to ask you to play lead for us. Basil said he could get us some good gigs. Maybe even a record deal if you're part of the package."

"I can't. Sneaking out for a night's one thing. There's no way I can hide regular rehearsals and gigs. And I think I might be missed if we spent a week in the studio recording."

"Trust me, Jon wants this more than anything."

A sinking feeling pinched her stomach. "Hey, wait, that's not the only reason he likes me?"

"Nah, he likes brunettes," Cal said, looking like he was considering whether to say more. "Be careful around my brother."

She could feel herself turning pink. "If I'd known everyone would be so interested in my love life, I'd have got one a lot sooner."

"Probably not my business." Cal leaned in, close enough so no one else could hear and waited for her to make eye contact. "He goes through girls fast."

"Maybe they just didn't understand him." *I do. He says so. Says he's never felt happy before like he does when he's with me. Says I'm different.* "Maybe you don't, either."

As she stomped off, she heard him mutter, "Don't understand my brother? Ooooooo-kay."

Dani crossed the campus, stopping short as she approached the locker she shared with Shelly. All the makeup in the world couldn't cover the bruise on Shelly's cheek.

"What happened?" She didn't need an answer.

Klutz, my hind end.

Stoner and one of his friends sat against the garage wall at Marc Stark's house, where Inferno typically rehearsed.

I still don't know Stoner's name.

The friend had introduced himself on the way over. Not that it mattered. His name wasn't important. His car was. Even if it was a rusted out Chevette. Stoner jumped at the opportunity to supply transportation when he'd heard Dani talking to herself about needing to get away from school early. Neither of the boys had bothered to ask why Dani wanted them to park the car out of sight.

Dani paced, madder with every step. An hour in, the hunk of junk pulled into the driveway.

Bobby had the nerve to ignore her, taking his sweet time getting out and unloading his gear, lighting a cigarette and pretending she wasn't scowling at him, hands on hips. She seethed, balled her fists, and waited until he tried to squeeze himself sideways through the door, guitar in one hand and amp in the other.

Stoner and his friend scrambled out of the way as she closed the gap between her and Bobby in three running steps, putting all that momentum and every ounce of her frame behind the fist that knocked him on his backside, cigarette smashed across his face, gear tumbling beside.

Bobby wiped blood from his split lip as Dani stood over him, pointed a finger in his face, and yelled, "My Daddy's a U.S. Marine, and he taught me lots more than that."

He curled into a ball as she kicked him in the ribs.

"Lay another hand on Shelly, and I'll show you more of it."

Bobby lay there in the fetal position as she spun on her heel.

"You two coming? Need you to help me find Jon so I can tell him we've fired our rhythm guitar player."

Chapter Eight

The next month was a blur for Dani. She hadn't seen Shelly since the night after she clocked Bobby. Shelly called that night in tears saying Bobby skipped town. It was all Dani's fault. How could she? Shelly hadn't been at school. Dani tried calling, but Shelly's mom always said she wasn't home. She'd tried going over, but no one would answer the door.

Vic wasn't making things any easier. *Doesn't he know I'm practically an adult? That I don't need him telling me who I can date or who I can hang out with?* Deep down, Dani knew he was just trying to do what Daddy would do, but that didn't make it any better.

Daddy. He'd be home soon after more than a month in military rehab facilities on the East Coast. When she finally got to talk to him on the phone, he'd backed Vic up—even when it came to her car, which still wasn't fixed. He didn't sound the same. He was always tired and couldn't talk long. She'd wanted to go to him, but he insisted she stay in school. Besides, she and Vic needed to keep the shop running.

Rio Flaco was planning to make a big thing of his homecoming. Throwing a parade and everything. Dani didn't know all the details, but Greg had told her the scuttlebutt was that he'd saved two Marines from being crushed to death by the Humvee that landed on his legs.

Dani didn't need a parade to tell her Daddy was a hero.

Hero or not, though, he took Vic's side on everything, especially Jon. Nothing she could say had been able to make either of them see sense and budge even a little. *They just don't understand him. At all. If they just got to know him, they'd see he's a good guy underneath it all, that he loves me, that I love him.*

Maybe someday, they'd see. For now, she'd have to continue keeping it quiet, seeing him when and where she could, even if that did mean only seeing him when she cut class to rehearse with Inferno. Her bandmates had quickly become like family to her.

It was no big deal. The school had sent notes about her absences, but she'd become pretty good at signing Vic's name. *It's not like I'm missing class enough to fail or anything.* Even if she did, she could afford to fail one class and still graduate. Two, as long as English IV wasn't one of them.

Jon wasn't thrilled with the reduced rehearsal time or the reduced make out time and made a point of saying so. Repeatedly. He didn't understand why Dani didn't just leave home if her brother gave her such a hard time. It wasn't like the cops were going to do anything about it this close to her eighteenth birthday. He had plenty of room in his trailer. She doubted that, though she'd never been inside. She knew in her gut that if she ever did, even for a few minutes, things would get out of hand. As it was, she'd stopped fighting it when he let his hands wander where they shouldn't, as long as he didn't try to take her clothes off.

She felt guilty about it, especially when she'd go to youth group and Kari would talk about purity—every week, it seemed. She did want to save herself for marriage, but she loved Jon. *How wrong can it be as long as we don't go all the way?*

Fortunately, most of their alone time consisted of a minute or two carved out of rehearsals while the rest of the band took a smoke break. What if they did go all the way? It wasn't any different than what everyone else was doing. Everyone but Kari, anyway. And Vic. And maybe a couple kids who didn't have any friends outside of youth group.

What would Mom say? Dani often found herself deep in the back of her closet, where she would run her hands over Mom's dress. It was still as white as in all the wedding pictures. Dani knew if Mom were here, she'd pull her close and tell her she was worth waiting for.

Vic allowed himself a smile as he reviewed the books. Everything was finally in order. Once Dad got home, Vic could turn the business side of things over to him. Dani and Greg could handle what they'd been handling all along, and there would be no real need for him in the shop. With the uptick in business Fidelis had experienced over the last couple months, they could even hire another guy if they needed to.

Things were even starting to cool down with Dani. She'd been on time to work every day. She'd been coming home on time from school. Most surprising, she'd stopped pushing the whole thing about going out with Jon. Dani had Dad's stubbornness, and he hadn't expected her to give in so easily. She seemed to be going out of her way to do everything he asked her to do. He debated whether he should tell her the parts for her GTO had been under his desk for two weeks.

He pulled a stack of brochures from his desk drawer and pored over them for the thousandth time. Missionary programs. He'd prayerfully narrowed his choices down to two, both of which would make use of his business education and experience while he served under a veteran missionary. Now it came down to deciding whether he felt called to South America or Central Africa. Being accepted to either involved a process, but at least he could get started on it now.

The first step, and the hardest, would be telling Dad. Dad had always been supportive of his preaching, but Vic was sure it had never occurred to him that he might have a bona fide calling to full-time ministry, much less missionary work. Dad had been talking about him taking over the business since before there was a business to take over.

A greasy cable landed on the desk, splattering the brochures and stacked ledgers.

"Found the problem with the Charger's speedometer."

Vic wiped a splotch of grease off his coveralls.

Greg leaned in, hands smudging the desk. Vic determined not to let him see how much that bugged him. He'd only get a rise out of it.

"Still got one more problem," Greg said.

"That problem went away for now."

"Wouldn't be so sure."

Vic arched his eyebrows, begging the question.

"How I know's not important. But that's not what I'm talking about. I was hoping to wait till Gunny got back, but I got an offer from a dealership up in Sacramento, and they need an answer. Hate to do it, but I got a kid to think about."

Vic leaned back, stacking the brochures. *This changes things.* He felt a migraine coming.

Chapter Nine

8 a.m. Saturday, Feb. 23, 1991
Rio Flaco Regional Airstrip

ani had never seen the town so worked up. President Bush had just declared the cease-fire two days ago, and everyone was excited to greet their very own war hero. Everywhere she looked, people waved flags and parents held small children to give them a better view. It looked like the whole town had turned out.

You'd think we'd lived here all our lives or something.

In reality, very few of these people outside of the church congregation even knew Daddy.

As the side door of the airplane opened, the Rio Flaco High School Band struck up "Stars and Stripes Forever" and what passed for a parade marched along the local airport's single landing strip.

Dani scanned the crowd for someone else as Daddy wheeled himself to the edge of the airstair's platform. *He said he'd be here.* She still debated whether asking him to come was a good idea. But if Vic and Daddy were ever going to give him a chance, she couldn't think of a better time to introduce them. *Maybe Jon thought better of it?* Kari stood on the other side of Vic, talking his ear off. He looked annoyed. *Maybe it's just as well.*

Daddy, in his dress blues, waved and saluted the crowd as a pair of uniformed Marines lifted him in his wheelchair. Best Dani could tell, he hadn't seen her yet. She waved her hands over her head, catching his eye and drawing a smile just as she felt warm hands touch her from behind.

Daddy maintained his smile, but his jaw set as he saw Jon encircle her waist, pull her back into himself, and kiss her ear, whispering something she couldn't make out over the noise. Dani smelled something under the cinnamon gum he chewed, faint but unmistakable. *Of all days. You promised you'd stop.*

Vic must have noticed the subtle change in Daddy's demeanor, too. Turning, he clenched his teeth and closed his eyes. Kari's jaw dropped, and she gave Dani a look over her glasses. Dani straightened to her full height, placing her hand over Jon's as if to dare either of them to say anything as the TV-9 camera crew panned back and forth between them and Daddy, a young reporter prattling on about local businessman and hero Gunnery Sergeant Anthony Grassigli and how his family waited for him just off the runway.

Vic made an obvious effort to paint a smile back on his face when the cameraman faced them.

"Here we are with Victor and Danielle Grassigli as they get ready to be reunited with their father after nine long months. And with Danielle is…"

Dani sported her sweetest smile, fighting the blush she felt coming. She'd planned this out, but now that the moment arrived, she feared she'd lose her nerve. She looked back over her shoulder at Jon. *Why are the rest of them here? And how dare they invite Bobby, of all people?*

"Ummm, this is Jon Ryder, my b—"

"Bandmate," Jon finished, pushing his way in front of her and mugging for the camera.

"He's the lead vocalist for Inferno," Bobby added. "Check out Dani and the rest of us at the Rock Creek Festival next Saturday."

"What're you doing, man?" Jon shoved Bobby.

Dani wanted to crawl under a rock. She watched disappointment work its way from Kari's eyes to her slumped shoulder and knew her days on the praise team were done. Now off to the side, Marc stood twirling a drumstick while Bobby Van Zie smirked and threw up the rock 'n roll salute. Beyond them, Tom Basil stood, trying to make conversation with Cal, who shuffled from foot to foot, shaking his head, eyes on the ground.

Vic stiffened, but forced a smile and made small talk with the reporter as their father wheeled closer, sunlight glinting off his brass and snorting fire as the Who's Who of Rio Flaco tried to keep up on his flanks.

Chapter Ten

Daddy sat at the table eating his oatmeal when Dani crawled out of her room the next day. She wasn't sure how he'd managed to dress himself, but he looked ready for church, his shirt and suit jacket as crisp as his dress uniform. A whiff of spray starch mingled with Brut aftershave brought comforting memories stretching back to her youngest days.

Dad sat ramrod straight and, even in his wheelchair, on eye level with her.

"About your friends." Daddy always did get right to the point.

"Friends wouldn't have done that." Dani tried to keep the sucking hole in the pit of her stomach out of her voice and put on a smile.

Daddy grunted, his jaw hard but his eyes soft.

"This band thing."

"I was trying to help a friend. I know that kind of music's not allowed, and I shouldn't have…"

"Just about killed your brother." Daddy reached under the table, setting the cassette carrier she'd hidden in her closet between them.

Dani felt heat rise up the back of her neck. "He had no right."

"He was worried." Daddy looked straight at her, waiting forever until she returned his gaze. "Should *I* be?"

Dani slumped into the chair across from him and looked away. Daddy's silence was worse than Vic's lectures. And she knew he'd sit there until she answered, no matter how long it took. "It's just music. I don't know. Probably. But not anymore. I'm done with that. Straight and narrow for me."

"About this guy."

Tears welled in Dani's eyes as she met her father's. She'd prepared herself for Daddy to be mad and didn't know what to make of his soft tone. He took her hands in his. She steeled her voice. "That song's over."

Daddy nodded slightly, grunting again. "You're old enough to make those choices." He sized her up as he slid the cassette carrier to her. "And these ones."

Did I just hear that?

"Thing about choices," Daddy said, looking away. "Every one you make will affect you."

"And other people," Dani sighed.

Vic went into the office before church Sunday morning to clear his things out of Dad's desk. Dad never let anything stop him long, and he intended to run his business—legs or no legs.

Suits me fine.

He had to admit Dani handled that whole weird scene well yesterday. She'd told that bunch of losers she'd been hanging around to get lost. For a minute, Vic thought he'd have to pull her off Shelly's big-mouthed boyfriend, but he tucked and ran before Dani got her hands on him. By the time Dad got to them, the Ryder brothers and their friends were in full retreat, crawling back to whatever hole they'd crawled out of. And while Dani was obviously upset, she kept it together for Dad's sake and even managed a smile for the cameras as Dad raced to them, his arms wide as the wheelchair covered the last ten yards.

No more was said of the issue last night. Whatever became of it, Vic was glad it wasn't on his shoulders anymore.

Vic tossed the grease-splattered missionary brochures on top of his box. *Won't be long now.* Still, he needed to pick his moment. Far as Dad knew, he still planned to stay on and eventually take over the business. Dad needed to know restoring cars wasn't in his plans, preferably soon enough so the shop could find a replacement by the end of summer.

"Better to restore souls," Vic said to himself.

"Some of us need it."

The voice startled Vic. It was the jerk who wrapped his arms around Dani yesterday.

❝Let's take your car," Daddy said.

Didn't he know?

"Keys are in it."

Dani wondered how he got the parts so quickly, to say nothing of who had done the work, but she wasn't about to argue. She opened the garage door so Daddy could maneuver onto the newly installed ramp. Before she could turn to heft him into the car, he opened the GTO's passenger door and managed to pull himself most of the way into the seat. One more grunt and his boots rested on the floorboard.

Dani double-checked to make sure the radio was tuned to the Christian station. Some song she'd never heard about the Lion of the Tribe of Judah. Her car gave a throaty growl as she shifted into gear. Daddy scowled when she hit the gas. *So sue me, I'm over-enthused.* In her peripheral, she caught the corners of his mouth relaxing into a smile as soon as he figured her eyes were on the road.

When they arrived, Daddy whistled low. Dani had never seen the church's parking lot so full and was sure Daddy hadn't, either. Fortunately, there were three handicapped spots open in the front row. Dani veered toward the nearest.

Daddy shook his head. "Park over there." He pointed to the few remaining spots nestled in the back of the lot.

Dani started to protest. Saw the set of his jaw. Thought better of it.

It took a full twenty-five minutes for Daddy to wheel himself through friends, acquaintances, well-wishers, and curious strangers, but he wouldn't let Dani push.

"Sorry we're late," Daddy said to Pastor Stenger as he wheeled through the front door five minutes before the service was set to start.

The preacher frowned slightly. "See that it doesn't happen again," he said, elbowing Daddy's shoulder and giving Dani a wink.

Dani followed behind Daddy's chair, marveling. She'd never seen the sanctuary more than half full. Kari brushed past, flanked by teenagers carrying extra chairs from the youth room.

"Oof!" Dani almost fell over Daddy's shoulder into his lap. Looking up, she saw what made him stop so suddenly.

Vic sat in the front pew, left side, where the family always sat. Next to him sat a smartly dressed redhead, her hair pulled into the tightest upside-down french braid Dani had ever seen. And on the other side of her, in ripped jeans and all his heavy metal glory, sat Jon.

I tried to get you to come to church for a month.

The veins on the back of Daddy's neck stood at attention. He wheeled in front of the pew, taking the spot next to Jon.

Sad? Hurt? Excited? Dani tried to define her emotional soup. *Mostly mad,* she decided. And lonely in a way she'd never known before. *That girl's the type Jon likes. Good girl type. Sure got over me fast.*

Jon hung his head as he extended his hand. "Mr. Grassigli."

Daddy grunted, eyes front. Dani wanted to crawl under the pew. She tried to be subtle when she elbowed him.

Daddy glanced over at her before turning to stare a hole in Jon. Jon winced, stifling a gasp as Daddy shook his hand. Jon looked like he wanted to catch her eye but didn't dare while Daddy maintained his grip. After what seemed a lot longer than it probably was, the Marine released the singer's hand. "Mr. Ryder."

Dani suppressed a smile, but as she watched Jon clench and unclench out of the corner of her eye, all she could think was *guess he won't be holding her hand for a while.*

ani tried paying attention to the service, but she couldn't help looking over at Jon and the redhead. A couple times, Jon leaned over and whispered something to the girl. Or maybe to Vic. Impossible to tell without being obvious.

Don't look at him, Dani. The service was ending, and all Dani could remember of the message was it had something to do with God not withholding any good gift.

Pastor Stenger invited hearers to come to the front to receive what he always called the greatest of gifts—salvation through Jesus Christ. Most parts of the service changed from week to week, but he always gave altar calls the same way. *Bet anyone that's been here more than a month could get up and give the altar call word-for-word if Pastor gave them the mic.* But Dani figured most of this morning's crowd was hearing it for the first time. Dozens made their way to the front to pray with Pastor Stenger, Kari, or one of the other church leaders.

Kari seemed distracted as she prayed for people, her pinched smile taking obvious effort. *Probably thinks that girl's with Vic.*

The redhead seemed to be ignoring Jon, who was staring at the floor. *Serves him right.* Vic leaned over and said something to the girl. She responded quickly, but without a hint of expression on her face.

Dani caught Jon looking over at her. *Lot of nerve while he's sitting with that other girl.* He averted his gaze back to the floor when he caught Daddy's eye. *Daddy doesn't have to be so mean.*

After the benediction, a crowd formed around Daddy. Dani knew he hated crowds, but he did his best to smile, nod, and shake hands. Jon stood hangdog on the perimeter. Despite her best efforts to stop it, her heart still skipped a beat when their eyes met. If she didn't know better, she'd swear by his look he was trying to apologize. *Doesn't matter. Nothing he could say would change yesterday or how he made me feel.* She wrestled with tangible emptiness.

Dani was glad when Kari pulled her away before the crowd thinned enough for Jon to get to her.

On the way to Kari's office, they passed the redhead. Vic sat an arm's length from her, explaining something, hands waving, pointing, forming signs like he always did when he was excited about something. Her face was still as stone. Kari swallowed hard but kept on.

Dani prepared herself for one of Kari's special made-to-order, one-on-one sermons as they stepped into the office. She was overdue for one. What she wasn't prepared for was Shelly, shaking.

Dani could still hear the crowd milling outside after Kari shut the door. She took a seat, looking around and trying to avoid Kari's eyes. Same knickknacks. Same books in the same spots on the same bookshelves. Same Integrity music from the same cassette player on the same corner table playing just loud enough to make out the lyrics if you strained. Same blue betta swimming lazily in the same glass bowl with the same frosted world map etched onto it. The only thing missing was Kari's everlasting smile, the one she didn't even take off when she was dressing you down.

Kari leaned back against her desk, arms crossed, glasses in hand, eyebrows knit. She closed her eyes. "I won't go into the reasons you shouldn't be running with that crowd right now."

Dani slumped her shoulders. *This is going to take a while.* Still, she found hope rising inside that she might be able to see Shelly again.

Shelly dabbed at the mascara making a beeline for her puffy cheeks.

"But since you've been running with that crowd..." Kari hesitated, looking like she was thinking through what to say next.

Kari always knows what to say.

"Where's Bobby?" Shelly broke in.

"Being a klutz, the last time I saw him."

Shelly looked at the ground, making no effort to stem the flow of tears. Dani regretted her sarcasm immediately, but this was the first time she'd seen Shelly without bruises in a long time.

Kari placed a protective hand on Shelly's shoulder and took a deep breath. "Everyone saw him with you yesterday."

"I saw him the same time everyone else did."

"He wasn't there announcing *my* band's concert," said Kari.

"I kicked him out of my…"

Kari raised her eyebrows, tilting her head.

Did I just call Inferno my band? To Kari Andersen? Don't start biting your lip, stupid.

"Look, I quit Inferno. Honest."

Shelly shot her a how-could-you look as Kari lowered her voice to just above a whisper. "Listen, Shelly really needs to find Bobby."

"She needs to find Bobby right now like I need another purity sermon."

Kari looked like she'd been slapped.

"Besides," Dani said, "I chased him off. Far as I know, he's skipped town."

"And I've skipped a period," Shelly said, allowing a moment for that to sink in. "I'm pregnant and I'm scared and I've been kicked out of my house and I don't know what I'm going to do and I just need to…" Shelly gasped for breath and let out a string of colorful words, bringing bright red to Kari's face and finishing with "find Bobby."

"Even if I knew where he was, you're better off without him." Dani softened her voice. "And so is the baby."

Dani reached to embrace her. Shelly recoiled.

"Jon probably knows where he is." *Lord, I'm not ready to talk to him. I can barely look at him.* "I'll ask."

ani sat outside the Starks' garage, head on the steering wheel. Jon had left the church by the time she got out of Kari's office, and Vic didn't know where he'd gone. He wasn't at his trailer, so Dani figured she'd find him here. *Who knows? Maybe Bobby, too.*

"Lord, I don't want to see either of them."

A tap on the car window. Basil. *Perfect. Wonder how long he's been standing there.* Her stomach turned. She shrugged the neckline of her blouse higher before cranking the window handle.

"Missed the applause?" he lit a match off the car door, taking a drag and leaning his arm on the window, allowing smoke to curl into the car.

"Just saying goodbye to the guys."

"Smart move."

Dani narrowed her eyes as he tamped ash from the cigarette.

Never going to get that smell out of my car.

Basil leaned in, resting his claw on her shoulder. "Drop 'em, kid. I'll have you filling stadiums in six months."

"Yeah, I'll be the next Lita Ford." Dani rolled her eyes, pulling away. "Singing duets with Ozzy and opening for Mötley."

"You'll make 'em forget all about Lita. And Joan. And Pat. And all the rest. Give me two albums, and I'll have Crüe opening for Dani Glass."

"What happened to Dani Grass?"

"Glass is better." He tamped the cigarette again, ash landing on her jeans. "More pure, but more dangerous. Fragile. Vulnerable. But it'll cut you. I'm telling you, you're a star, kid."

Dani closed her eyes. He did paint a picture. She felt the rush of the bar crowd, tried to imagine multiplying it a hundred, a thousand times over. The tingling worked its way to her toes.

Inferno's rhythm section shocked her from her dream, blaring from inside the garage. It sounded like they were working on the complex bridge she'd added to "Straight to the Top," one of Jon's better originals.

"Jon know you're out here?" Dani slid away, adjusting her top against Basil's stare. She let herself out the passenger side and headed inside.

Marc and Cal were just starting to nail the bridge, Cal's shoulder-length locks sporting a new perm, when Dani peeked in. She giggled in spite of herself, biting down on her lip. *Don't say anything; he's going to look like a poodle for six months.*

Marc had worked up a sweat, his T-shirt hanging from one of his cymbal stands. Keeping a solid beat with one hand, he pointed a drumstick at Bobby's Les Paul, leaning against the stacked amps.

Dani waved him off.

Marc leaned into a boom mic. "Baby, baby, baby, pleeeeeeeeeeeease…"

It was the first time she'd heard him sing. *Not bad.* She laughed and strapped on the guitar. *If nothing else, it'll tick Bobby off if he finds out.*

By the time Dani reached the second measure, Cal and Marc kicked their playing into another gear. One more time and they nailed the bridge, sailing into the climactic chorus. Seamless. Dani noticed her pink nail polish flaking onto the fretboard as she played the finger tap solo. She tapped harder.

Marc was still pounding out the big finish when Dani turned to Cal.

"Where's your brother?" she said.

"Not my turn to watch him."

"Bobby?" She set his guitar down, making sure to put it in a different place than she'd found it.

"Comes and goes as he pleases," Marc said, one of his twirling drumsticks getting away from him and clattering to the floor. "We're a better band with you anyway. C'mon back."

Dani looked at Cal. Cal looked away. Fishing a lavender pick embossed with a silver butterfly out of her pocket, she slid it between the Les Paul's strings.

Marc chuckled. "Jon would take you back."

Cal shot him a shut up look.

"What? She's all he talks about."

Dani bit her lip, chewing on that. "Not at the airport."

"So he's a jerk," Marc said. "It's lead singer syndrome."

"I don't think I could be just his bandmate."

"I've never seen him so into anyone," Marc said.

"Other than himself." Cal funked a bass riff, flipping his head to bounce the curls out of his eyes. "Look, I don't blame you. He doesn't deserve you."

"But you gotta play one more show with us." Marc's smile faded and, for the first time she'd seen, he looked serious.

"Here's the thing," Cal said, hesitantly. "Basil said if you don't play, we're done. And even if we could talk him out of it, we've got no show without you. Bobby's MIA."

"I'm twenty-six, Dani, and I still live with my parents." Marc pleaded and laughed at the same time. "If we don't get this deal, I'll have to cut my hair and learn to ask if you want fries with that. Can your conscience handle that?"

"What good will playing one show do?" Dani shook her head. But, truth be told, she didn't want that on her conscience.

While Dani looked for Jon in the Starks' garage, Vic looked at him across his desk in the Fidelis Garage.

"Can't believe I lost her." Jon stared at the floor, slurping black coffee from a Styrofoam cup, his eyes less bloodshot than they'd been this morning.

"Can't believe you had her." Maybe this guy wasn't as bad as he seemed. Looked like he was paying attention to Pastor Stenger this morning. He'd said the sermon was still on his mind.

"You got nothing to worry about," the singer blew hair out of his eyes, giving half a chuckle. "She's a good girl."

Vic rapped a crescent wrench on the desktop. "Good girls fall for bad boys all the time." *Like every girl I've ever been interested in.*

"I just wanted a guitar player." Jon looked away.

Is he choking back tears?

"Didn't mean to fall for her."

Vic considered going over all the things that were wrong with that kind of music and why Dani shouldn't be around that scene to begin with, why it wasn't fit for pigs' consumption. But it looked like God might be working on Jon's heart. And Vic knew he had scared people off by coming on too strong about worldly music and movies and stuff like that in the past. *Maybe a different approach would be better.*

Vic retrieved an old burgundy leather Bible from the drawer and flipped it open to the page marked with a frayed ribbon. Turning it around, he pointed to a verse he'd highlighted in yellow and underlined in red the year he'd first started reading the Scriptures.

Jon leaned in, focusing bleary eyes. "Be ye not unequally yoked together with unbelievers." He scrunched his forehead as Vic motioned for him to go on. "For what fellowship hath righteousness with unrighteousness? And what communion hath light with darkness?"

Vic sat back, steepling his fingers and silently studying Jon.

"What concord hath Christ with Belial?" Jon stammered, face scrunched. "Who's Belial?"

"It means Dani shouldn't be dating you," Vic said, drawing in a deep breath. "If you're not following Christ, it'll force her to choose between walking in the light and running with the devil."

"You calling me the devil?"

Vic stood, leaning over the desk as close as he could and waiting for the rocker to make eye contact through his sheepdog bangs. "If you love her, you won't put her in that position."

Chapter Eleven

A few days later, Dani heard Daddy's voice from the garage but couldn't make out what he was saying. He seldom raised his voice. Not even with his Marines. He never needed to. She eased the door open, sliding in.

"... doesn't want to see you. And I'd better not." Daddy slammed the phone.

She considered waiting, giving him a minute. He didn't get mad, but when he did, it was best to steer clear until the dust settled. Never took long. But she had to know.

He smiled over his newspaper when she walked around the corner. "Didn't hear you."

She tilted her head, hoping to avoid having to ask directly.

Daddy grunted. Pointed to the paper. "War's over. Officially. We won."

Dani raised an eyebrow and put on a half-smile. "Changing the subject's my trick."

Daddy flashed the same lopsided grin he'd sported for a solid week the year before he finally broke down and got her the puppy for her birthday. True enough, that was the one year she hadn't wheedled the secret out of him early. But birthday presents were the last thing on her mind.

"Oh yeah, that's coming up," she said, shrugging it off and kissing him on his balding forehead.

"Big year." He beamed. Dani always loved it when Daddy looked at her like that.

"All grown up." She shrugged and sat on his lap, putting an arm around him. She scrunched her face, crinkled her nose, and looked him deep in the eyes, putting on her best Daddy's little girl. Whispered. "Grown up enough to tell boys to get lost all by myself."

He reddened. Stiffened. Held her tighter.

"How many times has he called, Daddy?" She tried not to smile as the warmth rose in her belly. She knew she was biting her lip. Didn't care.

Daddy sat ramrod straight, a slight squint. A demeanor she'd seen him take a thousand times around his Marines. "We have company coming for dinner."

"I was planning to…"

Daddy locked eyes, head tilting a fraction of a hair.

"Yes, sir."

After checking the pasta, Vic gave the sauce a quick slurp. Felt his lip twitch. *Needs to be perfect.* It would have been nice to have his sister's help, but she was off in her room sulking. *Ah well, Dad gets to worry about that now.* He considered his options. Maybe a pinch more of this? A dash more of that? He looked through the spice rack, humming, convinced Mom had shared some secret ingredient with Dani. He remembered Mom always putting more garlic in the sauce than the recipe called for, but he shook that idea off. *You never know.*

Dad hadn't said much since Vic got home from the shop. He'd sat in the den, looking through those old scrapbooks Mom used to make and playing chess with himself. It wasn't like Dad to wear his sentiments on his sleeve anyway, but lately, he was retreating into himself even more than usual. *Just hope he's himself at dinner. Wonder what he'll think.*

Ten minutes later, the doorbell rang. Vic looked at his watch as the minute hand made its move to the top of the dial. Precisely six.

Vic barely recognized the young woman at the door. It was Julie, no doubt about that. Same pale green eyes that seemed to take in everything. But her copper hair framed her face, falling over her shoulders and catching glints of sunlight. He found himself slack-jawed.

"You going to let me in, or do I need to call the dogs again?" Her tone flat, Vic searched her eyes for some sign she was kidding. Nothing.

He nodded toward the dining room where Dad was wheeling himself into place. Dani slouched in the next chair, gazing out the window like she was watching for someone. She half-acknowledged Julie when Vic pulled out her chair and made introductions.

"So, Vic tells me he found you on the side of the road." *There goes Dad trying to be a comedian.* It was something, at least.

Julie let it hang in the air a moment before deadpanning, "The official report differs in some respects."

Vic relaxed as Dad tried to suppress a smile. Dad lobbed a few more lame attempts at humor, and Julie returned every serve without the least expression. Things were going perfectly.

Then Dani stopped playing with her food and chimed in.

"Can I be excused? I need to go find Jon and Bobby."

All humor drained from Dad's face.

"I promised Shelly."

If it was possible, Dad sat up straighter.

"And Kari."

Dad cut his eyes toward Vic.

Vic shrugged. *Don't ask me.* He looked over at Julie. If the outburst bothered her, she didn't show it.

"It'll wait." Dad's end-of-discussion tone.

"I won't know where they are later." Dani wheedled, fidgeting. "Right now, they're at the Starks', rehearsing."

"Marc Stark?" Julie asked.

Dani nodded.

"From Inferno?"

Another nod.

"You should stay away from there," Julie said, as unemotionally as everything else she said.

Dani raised an eyebrow, like she usually did when she was looking to argue. Dad leaned in.

Julie seemed to pick up the unasked questions. She shook her head slowly, tight-lipped. "Call it a professional opinion."

"You don't even know them!" Dani said. Vic wondered whether the tone and the groan that followed were meant for Julie or Dad.

Julie studied Dani passively as Dad started to rise, realized he couldn't, and sat back into his chair, grunting in Dani's direction. Dani shoved herself from the table, slamming the garage door on the way out.

"Julie, I'm…" Vic started, through clenched teeth.

She waved him off as Dani's car roared to life, tires squealing.

Seconds later, Dani appeared back in the door, head hanging, the smell of burned rubber following her into the house.

"I'm sorry." She avoided everyone's eyes, especially Dad's, as she sloughed toward her room. "That was uncalled for."

Julie turned back to her pasta.

Chapter Twelve

The next Saturday, Dani headed to the Rock Creek Festival. After the scene she'd caused the other night, she was surprised she'd been allowed out of the house. Daddy hadn't said much about it, really.

Dani hadn't told anyone she was coming here. Even the band wasn't expecting her. *Wonder what Jon's gonna think?*

The car parts she'd told Daddy she was going to LA to get were safely in her trunk already. She hated lying to Daddy, but there was no way he'd have let her come here. And she couldn't think of any other way to keep her promise to Kari and Shelly. This was the only place she knew for sure Bobby would be. Besides, it wasn't right to let Cal and Marc down.

"It's just one more time," she told herself as she turned into the fairgrounds. *After this, no more lies.* Inferno would have to make it or break it on their own. *Vic and Daddy are right. Jon's no good for me, no matter how much it aches to admit. After this, my guitar is for the Lord and Him only. No more playing both sides of the road.* Kari always said you only end up hurt that way. The fact that Kari was right stung almost as much as knowing she couldn't be with Jon anymore. *No way I'll ever feel that special again.*

"But it's undivided devotion for me from now on, Lord. Just get me through this one last thing."

Dani navigated around Warrant's tour bus behind the main stage to the pair of smaller stages where local bands and B-listers set up, tuned up, or waited with their gear. When she finally found Inferno's gear, Bobby leaned against the crates talking to Tom Basil. It looked like Basil was doing most of the talking, though it was impossible to tell with the two facing away. *Not looking forward to this.* Beyond them stood Marc and Cal. Cal looked fit to be tied. *Where's Jon?* She wasn't sure if she wanted to see him.

"Don't matter where Jon is," Basil said as she came into earshot and the first act ran their sound checks. "Shouldn't have to tell you people twice."

"C'mon, man, we're already booked." Bobby looked up and saw her coming. Shook his head. Spat.

"No girl, no show."

"Look, man, she quit."

"She quit hiding," Dani said, turning Basil on his heels. "Let's tune up."

Bobby stormed off, muttering something about chicks and trouble.

"Knew you'd come," Cal said as Marc twirled his sticks and sported a mile-wide grin.

She tossed them her keys. "Gear's in the trunk."

Just the two of them now, Basil leered. "Let's hope Jon stays lost."

Dani rolled her eyes.

"You wearin' that?"

Her outfit didn't exactly scream heavy metal, but what was she supposed to do? Tell Daddy she was going to buy car parts in fishnets and a leather mini? *As if I have anything like that in my closet anyway.*

She walked away, finding the spot where Jon's gear was stacked. Plopping into his folding chair, she cocked her head. *That a Bible on his amp?* She reached over. It was one of Vic's old bibles, open to First Corinthians 13. Verse 7 was freshly highlighted: "Love always protects, always trusts, always hopes, always perseveres." In the margins, in Jon's messy handwriting, her name was scrawled in a heart.

She set it back down. *Okay, so he's reading the Bible. Great. Doesn't mean he's good for me. But what if he's really taking it to heart? Anyone can change. Kari preaches that all the time. Even Vic believes it. No. Good for him. Vic talked him into Jesus. That doesn't change what he did at the airstrip.* Dani choked down the hollow ache spreading from her middle. *Just do the show, talk to Bobby, and get out of here.*

V ic strolled along the tree-lined path. It had taken a while for him to build up the nerve to reach for Julie's hand, and he was surprised by how small and warm it felt in his. The aroma of fresh-baked cinnamon bread wafted from the picnic basket on her other arm, mixing with fresh pine. The chirping of late morning birds was interrupted by the sound of a distant electric guitar being tuned.

Vic hadn't realized there was an outdoor concert here today or he'd have suggested meeting somewhere else. Julie assured him she didn't mind. They could hear the show without paying to get into the gated areas. Said she liked Warrant. That didn't exactly earn her any points. *Ah well, that'll change when she comes to faith in Christ. Give her some time.*

Vic tried to make eye contact with her as they walked and talked, but she kept eyes front until they found a shady spot in the picnic area. *Perfect place for getting to know each other better.*

"Wouldn't have pegged you for baking," Vic said. If possible, the cinnamon bread smelled even sweeter than Mom's.

"From scratch." He thought he caught a hint of a smile, though her eyes were as inexpressive as ever, her tone flat.

Brunch passed with small talk. Vic asked about her family. She changed the subject.

The picnic area started to fill as some local band scratched out what passed for music in the distance. By the time noon rolled around and the second band took the stage, the rolling sea of teens and twenty-somethings made real conversation impossible. The stage was out of sight from here, but that didn't stop the sound from assaulting them.

Julie didn't seem to mind, twitching her shoulders in time to the music. She glanced at him from time to time, the same look she'd given when she pulled him over.

Glad she doesn't have her radio.

She hopped up, grabbing Vic's hands as the band wrapped up their set with a lousy cover of Van Halen's "Dancing in the Street."

I don't even listen to this kind of stuff. But Vic got up and rocked, stiff-legged, more or less in time to the music as she swayed closer, further away. *She's done this before. She's good.*

"Vic?!" A familiar voice.

He looked over his shoulder and let go of Julie's hand as Kari wove through the crowd.

obby returned with Jon just in time for sound check. Dani tried not to look at him. Her heart sank every time she glanced, only to see him looking away. *Just as well. Only make it harder anyway.*

Basil lumbered over, motioning the band to huddle up as the emcee worked the crowd. Dani stood apart as the others gathered. She turned away, but the hair standing on the back of her neck told her Basil was still leering.

"Don't care what else you play, close with the chick's version of "Mind in the Gutter."

"I'm not asking her to…" Jon sputtered.

"Got three other bands I can book."

Bobby grunted. "Who cares if she don't like singing it? Make her sing or go home."

"She don't play, you got nothing. Just a dime-a-dozen garage band with a Vince Neil look-alike."

When Dani looked back at the band, Jon was still looking away. Cal stood behind him, shaking his head while Marc clasped his hands. Praying? Pleading?

Bobby slammed the rest of his beer and walked over to Dani, "Look, I know…"

A knot formed in her stomach. Jon still wouldn't look at her.

"Let's just get it over with," she said. "We need to talk after the show." *I just hope no one in the crowd knows me.*

"What are you doing here?" Vic asked.

Kari's eyes fired the question back at him as she waved a handful of cartoon gospel tracts. Her eyes darted to Julie. Vic couldn't remember the last time he'd seen Kari without her trademarked smile.

"Didn't know there was a show till I got here." Vic looked back and forth between the women. *Why am I feeling guilty? I don't owe her an explanation.* If he hadn't known Kari, he probably wouldn't have noticed her eyes narrow. Julie maintained eye contact, not appearing to think much of it.

"Join us." Julie's voice was as neutral as ever, but Vic couldn't help thinking she hoped the invitation would be turned down. "There's plenty."

Conversation stopped as the emcee announced the next band—Inferno. Vic was no audio expert, but he noticed the sound quality coming from the distant amplifiers had improved markedly. Less garbled. Also louder.

"Let's go." He knelt, stuffing leftovers back into the picnic basket. "I know another spot across town. Quieter."

Julie gave half a shrug, still appearing to size Kari up. "I wouldn't want my sister hanging out with them, but they're not a bad band. Think I'll stay. You two can go if you want."

Vic caught his breath, felt his eyebrows raise. *Is that a glimmer of hope in Kari's eyes?* He'd dared to believe Julie was starting to like him. *So she listens to this stuff. That'll pass. Just need to get her saved.* But if Julie cared whether he stayed or went, she wasn't showing it. *Wish I could make myself like Kari like I like Julie. Be a lot more convenient.*

Offering a strained smile, Kari stashed the tracts in her purse. "Guess it won't hurt to stay awhile. I didn't get your name last Sunday."

Vic's head throbbed as he sat back down between the two. He rubbed his temples as Jon's distinct scream pierced from the distant speakers straight to his brain, singing Van Halen's "And the Cradle Will Rock." Vic did his best not to bob his head to the song. He'd known every word to everything Van Halen sang before he came to Christ.

As the song continued, Julie and Kari danced around the pleasantries. He silently prayed for Jon. How anyone could listen to this stuff, much less sing it, after they'd been saved was beyond him. He knew Kari felt the same. They'd talked about it often enough. *At least I don't have to come home to hear Dani blasting it and turning it off when I get home like I'm some kind of idiot who wouldn't notice anymore. Not since Dad came home.*

Vic strained to hear better when the band hit the chorus. For a second, he thought he recognized one of the backing voices. *Impossible.*

obby glared at Dani as she laid into the opening solo of "Hit the Door Running." Basil had begrudgingly consented to allow them to follow their opener with a pair of Inferno's originals. Dani felt the rest of the band holding their breaths, waiting to see how the crowd would react. She dropped to her knees, bending the strings till they almost popped, allowing the last note to invade the space. The crowd erupted as she leaped to front center stage, the band kicking into the groove behind her, the front row reaching out, grasping at the fringes on her jeans as she strutted, teetering across the edge. She tried to breathe, drinking in the adulation.

Is this what it's like to be high?

She closed her eyes as Jon jumped into the opening lyrics:

> *"Momma always said I was a crazy child,*
> *Daddy always said that boy has gone buck wild,"*

The undeniable chemistry she'd felt the first time they played together coursed through her veins, her heart fluttering, beating time for his voice. *Don't look at him, Dani. Don't do it.*

"Get in my way, I'll knock you to your knees
If you're gonna come along, we're gonna do what I please
And when I've finished with you
And it's time to leave...
I'm gonna hit the door runnin'
Got no time to stop
Gonna hit the door runnin'
For all I've got
Gonna hit the door runnin'
And I won't bother looking behind..."

As the band hit the last note, coming to the cold close, Dani ventured her first look at Jon, hoping despite herself he'd be looking back. *He has to miss me a little, right?* His back to her, he poured every ounce of energy into the crowd. *That's okay. All part of being the front man.*

She kept her eyes glued to him through the next song, watching every sway, every slide as he worked the crowd. She knew he could feel her in the music, knew it with every note she dragged out of her Strat. Knew it even though he never looked at her. Once, twice, she thought he was going to. He looked far enough stage left she could see the blue in his eyes but turned away before she could make eye contact.

Dani tried moving closer to Jon on the stage, but Cal stepped between them, slapping, popping, and dragging the bass cord into her path. She'd move, he'd move, always keeping himself between her and his brother. Sidling shoulder to shoulder, she stared him down and mouthed, "Move!"

He didn't.

❝All right, Rock Creek!" Jon's shout carried across the park as the last notes of a searing guitar solo faded. Vic could only imagine how loud it must be in the gated area. "That's Dani Glass, and we're gonna give her the mic for this next song!"

Vic and Kari exchanged open-mouthed looks as a guitar riff crunched and Dani's sultry rasp—the one Kari kept telling her not to use in church—beckoned every man in earshot:

> *"So I'm not the kind of girl*
> *That you think I should be,*
> *Take a second look*
> *You just might get what you see…"*

Vic wasn't sure whether his face was pale or crimson, but he felt the blood rush, then drain from it. Almost in a haze, he saw Julie motion for him to sit back down.

> *"I got my mind in the gutter…"*

Vic hit his feet running. Kari called, her voice lost in the crowd as Dani's voice soared above it.

> *"My mind in the gutter…"*

Vic pinballed through the crowd. The main gate. Neon yellow shirt. Security guard.

"Move it!"

"Got a ticket, bud?"

> *"My mind in the gutter and my body ain't far behind…"*

"My sister's…"

The guard looked bored. "She can't get in without a ticket, either."

"I got my mind in the gutter…"

I'm bigger than him. Vic blew past.

"And I'm eager to please…"

Vic shook the man off as he tried to grab his shirt.

The security guard yelled something at his back as Vic rushed through the crowd.

"Got my mind in the gutter…"

Some moved. Some pushed back. The crowd pressed forward, arms extended to grope his baby sister. Something hit the back of his head. Again, harder. The last thing Vic heard as everything went black was Dani belting over the erupting crowd:

"C'mon and get a little dirty with me!"

The crowd continued shouting, screaming, raising general pandemonium while Dani cornered Bobby backstage.

"Look, thanks for playing." Bobby turned his back. "Now go away."

"Listen, Daddy." Dani grabbed his shoulder and turned him around. "We need to talk."

Bobby shot her a dirty look.

"Get used to it, Daddy." The crowd's volume rose to the point she doubted he heard her, so she repeated herself, louder.

"Sounds like we gotta go back out." Bobby strapped his Les Paul back on and shouldered past her.

"Didn't you hear me, *Dadd-y?*"

"Been called lots of things by groupies. That one's new. And weird." He headed onstage, calling behind, "But hey, skip the encore. We're better without you."

Bobby pulled back the curtain separating them from the stage but retreated after peeking through, shaking his head in disgust. From the other side, Dani heard along with everyone else:

"Um, yeah, okay. I've got one more."

An acoustic guitar strummed slowly, with the mixture of conviction and mediocre musicianship that marked Jon's playing. "Gonna let the band sit it out. Probably should have played this one first. Wrote it yesterday and it might be the only chance I get to sing it to the girl I wrote it for:

> *When I met you*
> *Oh, I wasn't in your plans,*
> *But your smile, your touch,*
> *Your gentle ways*
> *I'm still tryin' to understand*
> *You looked at me,*
> *I felt a love, girl,*
> *Like I've never known*
> *And I'm telling you the truth,*
> *I was afraid to let it show*
>
> *And you said, "Love is patient,"*
> *But I just might need a little help*
> *I'm down here on my knees, I'm begging,*
> *Tryin' to save myself*

I'll say a thousand times I'm sorry, girl,
To make you see
I'm daring to dream
You'll come back and walk with me

So, take my hand,
You'll see more than just the show,
Lean on me, just lean in close
Doesn't matter where we go
'Cause love protects,
Yeah, true love hopes,
They say it never fails
I can't live without you, girl...
Don't leave me to myself
'Cause you said, "love is patient,"
But I just might need a little help
I'm down here on my knees, I'm begging,
Tryin' to save myself
I'll say a thousand times I'm sorry, girl,
To make you see
I'm daring to dream
You'll come back and walk with me.

When Vic opened his eyes, haze covered everything. Someone had plopped him in a lawn chair. He could make out Jon Ryder singing over the ringing in his ears. A few steps away, a fuzzy Julie talked with three, four... no, just two blurry police officers. His head felt like he had whacked it on an undercarriage. Repeatedly. He touched the knot throbbing on the back of his head. Big mistake. Pain shot clear to his toes, and everything started getting blurrier again.

"Looks like your boyfriend's waking up."

Vic's eyes cleared enough to see the playful shove Julie gave the officer as he and his partner walked back out into the crowd. *Don't have time for this.*

"Whoa!" Julie pushed him gently back into the chair.

"Gotta get Dani."

"Gave my word you'd let it go. C'mon, let's get you home."

He took her hand, taking a step toward the stage area in the general direction the music came from.

"Got the cuffs if I need them."

Was she smiling? Hard to tell with his head spinning.

"Where'd Kari…?"

"Gone." So was Julie's smile.

ani hid behind the band's gear, head spinning and trying to focus on what she'd come here to do. She'd kept up her end with Cal and Marc, and only one thing remained—make sure Bobby understood Shelly carried his baby.

But have you ever heard anything so beautiful? "I knew he still loved me." She dabbed at her eyes. *Don't want to be a mess when I see Jon.*

She peeked around the corner while the crowd went wild at the emcee announcing Warrant. The band huddled, wrapped in a heated conversation that didn't seem to interest Jon as Warrant fueled the crowd's fire with "All My Bridges are Burning."

His eyes met hers. A half smile.

Am I that obvious? Stop biting your lip, Dani. And make him come to you.

Jon finally broke himself away from the others, over Bobby's lewd objections. Dani leaned over the amp cases, chin resting on the backs of her hands. She lost herself in his eyes as he stopped a step short, smiling ear to ear, eyebrow cocked in an unasked question.

How can I tell him no? Remember what he highlighted? And that song... no way Vic or even Kari could say he's bad for me now.

She tilted her head toward his, closing her eyes as he took the final step, wrapping her in his arms. The world seemed to fade as she waited. *Is he teasing me? Not like him to hold back without being told. Firmly. Or maybe he's changing? Maybe this is respect? How's he supposed to kiss you while you're biting your lip anyway?* She leaned forward to give him a little nudge.

Whump!

Tom Basil stood beside them, pointing a silver pen at a stack of typewritten pages he'd slammed on top of the cases. Jon held her hand, but his eyes were on Basil. Basil's eyes were on her.

With her free hand, she fastened her top button.

"All standard stuff," Basil said, handing Jon the pen.

Jon's jaw dropped to his knees as the rest of the band gathered round.

"Not you." Basil pointed the pen toward Bobby. "Nobody's using two guitars anymore."

Bobby narrowed his eyes and bit hard on his lip. She was surprised he didn't draw blood as he muttered obscenities directed at her.

"I'm not signing anything." She put her hands up.

Jon looked up from signing.

Dani felt every eye on her. "This was my last show."

Basil picked up the contract and turned to Jon. "No girl, no record, no tour."

"Come on, Dani. These chances don't come every day." Jon's eyes pleaded. "If you love me..."

Dani looked up at him, playing with his shirt buttons. "I have to finish school." She couldn't believe it, but now she was pleading.

Bobby erupted into profanity. Somewhere among the four-letter words, Dani heard, "We don't need her."

Jon looked back and forth between Dani and Bobby. "You're my best friend, but…"

Basil stood firm. "Dani's version of "Mind in the Gutter" goes on the record, or there's no record."

Jon frowned. Bobby made a lewd gesture and walked away, the stacked cymbals crying foul as Bobby kicked his Les Paul into them. Marc added his objection when Bobby shoved over the drum cases.

"How much does this pay?" Dani's voice barely rose above a whisper.

Basil pointed to the number.

"I'm in," Dani said, taking the pen.

"That-a-girl," Basil said. "Sign right there."

Bobby stopped cold in the middle of a tirade that could have made Daddy's Marines blush and picked up his guitar, raising it over his head to smash it.

"But only if Bobby is," Dani said, shock registering on Jon and Basil's faces as Bobby lowered his guitar.

"I'll have to think about it," Bobby said.

Jon grabbed him by his collar and shook him.

Bobby shoved back, toppling the singer. "Thirty seconds ago, we were 'friends, *but.*' You were gonna throw me away for rent-a-chick."

Dani couldn't believe he'd call her that to her face. Apparently, Cal couldn't, either. He stepped up, taking a wild swing that Bobby dodged, laughing scornfully.

"Stop it!" Dani looked at Cal as Jon picked himself off the ground. Marc held Cal back as she turned her attention back to Bobby. "You're going to need the money, Daddy."

Bobby cocked his head. Dani imitated him, drawing a blank stare. She cradled an imaginary baby.

"It's called child support."

Bobby squinted. "Ain't even kissed you yet."

"Uh… Shelly?"

"Probably not mine."

Dani balled her fists.

He took a step back. "Okay, okay… if it is, couple hundred bucks should take care of it." He pulled a wad of bills from his wallet. "Here, you give it to her."

Dani couldn't believe what she was hearing. "Shelly would never. You need to call her."

"So, about those signatures…" Basil ruffled the contract.

Chapter Thirteen

Saturday, March 16, 1991
Alley Kat Recording Studio, Los Angeles

"Just saying I could get you further up the card if you had a decent light show," Basil said as the band took five.

Dani rolled her eyes. *Can we just get this over with? If I have to sing "Mind in the Gutter" one more time, I'm going to scream.*

"What's wrong with what we have?" Jon's eyes were bloodshot.

"Don't look at me," Marc said. "My parents want me out of the basement as it is. Mom's been bringing home job applications."

Basil cast lustful eyes at the Les Paul.

"Don't even think about it," Bobby said.

"You were gonna smash it when you were out. Now you can't part with it?" Basil ran a hand through greasy wisps of hair as he tapped ash from his cigarette onto the floor. "I could get ten grand for it. Get you a Peavey and a good used light show. Got a buyer lined up."

"The rest of us are all-in," Jon said.

"*Can't* sell it," Bobby said through gritted teeth.

"Not like it's sentimental," Jon smirked. "You got it—"

Bobby's glare cut him off.

Jon held his hands up. "Not like anyone would find out. Or care. Heard Nikki Sixx got his first guitar the same way."

"Was it a classic Gibson with an early serial number?"

"*You just got lucky,*" Jon sang. "Heck, you didn't even know what you had until Dani made a fuss over it."

Bobby shook his head. "Not happening."

"Welcome to the bottom of the card, folks," said Basil, "where you get bad sound mixing, and you play to a bunch of empty seats while the crowd buys beer and T-shirts from other bands before the real show."

"C'mon, they don't really mess with the soundboard, do they?" Jon asked.

"If they didn't, my band would still be cutting hit records, and I wouldn't be here babysitting you." Basil sat back, rubbing his chin. "Unless you can talk Dani into making real nice with the sound guys, you'll be lucky to get half power."

Bobby grunted. "She don't even do that for Jon."

Dani backhanded Jon's arm, shaking her head at both of them and finding a stool on the other side of the room. *What business is it of Bobby's what we do—or don't do?*

"About that," Basil said, "I don't give a flying flip what you do in your trailer, but in public, this ain't happening."

Jon walked over and put his arm around Dani. "I'm not hiding being with her. Got nothing to be ashamed of."

If you didn't include the occasional need to remind him of where his hands shouldn't be, Dani agreed.

"You want a crowd? Don't let anyone in the audience think Dani's off the market."

"What difference does it make?" Jon said. "We don't get that light show…"

"I have an idea," Dani said, snuggling into him. "But first, we have to get this record done. I'm running out of excuses to come down to LA on Saturdays."

That evening, Vic sat across a small glass-top table from Julie on the balcony of her apartment, paper plates in front of them. *I like women looking like women, but man, she looks good dressed down.*

"Not much of a cook," Julie admitted, handing over a bottle of ketchup, "but I can burn a burger. And the o-rings are my father's special recipe."

"What about the cinnamon bread?"

"Grew up in my dad's bakery. But mostly we ate out."

It was the first time she'd mentioned her parents. "I'd love to meet your dad and mom."

Julie closed her eyes, inhaled sharply, looked away.

Bad subject? Her eyes are misty.

She went inside, lingering at the fridge before returning with a pair of Coke cans, eyes clear and dry.

Vic prayed and took his first bite, smiling. Burned felt like an understatement. "Burger's good."

"Ketchup covers a multitude of sins."

Sins. I really shouldn't be here alone with her. Could look wrong. I wouldn't let Dani do it. But that's different. I'm an adult. And we're not doing anything we shouldn't.

She nibbled onion rings in silence, no ketchup. Vic felt like she was studying him as he made lame attempts at small talk.

"They tell me Mom left when I was four." Her voice was even flatter than usual. "I don't remember her. Dad—I don't want to talk about my dad right now."

Vic took her hand in both of his, feeling like he should say something, silently praying. He squirmed as the silence dragged on, but words escaped him.

Finally, she turned her eyes to him and leaned in. They were undoubtedly misting now, though it looked like she tried to fight it.

"Thank you," she said, putting her arms around his neck and pressing her lips to his.

Every cell in Vic's body shouted, refusing to shut up even after she'd pulled herself away. He'd kissed a few girls, but never quite like this. And now she stared up at him, looking like a little girl, a tear dripping freely down her cheek as she pulled his face down to hers again.

The kiss lingered forever. She moved her hand to his waist.

Vic froze. Pulled back. Shook. "I need to go."

"You're not mad?" she whispered as he stepped away from her.

"I'm... it's just..." Vic shook his head, trying to bring himself back down to earth as he headed to the door. "I'll call you."

"Sure you will," she said under her breath as he slipped out.

The next morning before church, Dani made coffee just the way Daddy liked it. How he drank the stuff, she couldn't fathom. She set his USMC mug in front of him as he sat down with the paper.

"About that band," she said, drawing a long, hard look. "We're really good."

"We?"

"If I'm in, they have a real shot."

"You're still in high school."

"Never stopped me from working before." Her turn to look him straight in the eye. *He can't deny I do my share around the shop.*

"Call that work?"

"Music's my whole life." She rested her head on his shoulder. "I was born to play guitar. You said so yourself when you got me my first real one. And you know how hard I've worked at it."

"So keep working hard and playing in the church band."

"I want to play my own songs. My own way."

"If Kari doesn't approve, why should I?"

"They're just songs, Dad. They're not that bad." *Drop the end off Daddy, he'll back down every time.*

"I don't know about this crowd you're hanging around."

"True, you don't know him."

"Him?"

"Give him a chance."

"I'd like to give him a haircut."

Dani returned his grin. "Don't you dare."

Note to self: hide the shears before Jon comes over.

Daddy drummed his fingers. "You'll be eighteen soon."

"Fifteen days."

"I'll let you keep playing with this band with a couple conditions."

"Anything!" *Don't come across so excited.*

"First, you don't let it stop you from enrolling in college."

"What if we're on tour?"

He sat on that a minute, probably sizing her up to see whether she was serious. Dani giggled and tossed her hair.

Should probably tell him. I want to. It's a bad idea.

He took a swig of coffee and conceded with a chuckle, "Sure, if you're on your world tour, I'll let it slide. But only till the tour's done. Second condition—"

The front door slammed.

"Vic?" she said. She'd only seen his face that flushed once.

"You all right, son?"

"I just... I need..." Vic held his hands up, beelining to his room.

Daddy waved Dani off and followed him.

7 a.m. Saturday, March 23, 1991
Fidelis Classic Restoration

The next Saturday, Vic opened the shop door and stepped aside, getting a kick out of the shock registering on Jon's face.

"Just the man I wanted to talk to." Dad spoke, almost inaudibly. In Vic's experience, when Dad lowered his voice, you'd better listen close.

"We're running late," Jon said, leaning against the door frame. "Dani here?"

"Sit," Dad said, quieter still.

Jon sat.

Vic stood over Dad's shoulder as Jon seemed to wilt under his glare. Dad rolled his wheelchair closer, inspecting the musician.

"Coffee."

Vic ducked into the office, returning with a pair of Styrofoam cups filled to the brim with the tar Dad brewed a couple hours ago. Jon looked like he was afraid to drink it.

Don't blame you.

Jon looked like he was trying not to squirm as Dad slurped and studied him.

"You've been seeing lots of Dani."

"She's—"

Dad raised his hand. Vic couldn't see his face. Didn't need to. Knew the look.

Jon shut up.

"I've allowed this band thing," Dad said, leaning forward and waiting for Jon to make eye contact. "But you won't be taking Dani anywhere today. We have a rule in our house about dating. First date is dinner. At our house."

Jon hummed and hawed for a long minute before taking a deep breath and a sip of the coffee. He made a face but took a second drink. "I didn't know. But I was just picking her up for rehearsal."

Is he being defensive? Afraid he might say something Dad doesn't already know? The dinner-at-our-house rule applied to Vic when he was in school, too. Whenever possible, he still brought dates home before taking them out.

"Nonnegotiable," Dad said.

"Fair enough." Jon shifted in his chair but maintained eye contact.

"Another thing—I won't tell her she can't play," Dad said, firing the next words off staccato. "But. You. Will. Not. Ask. Her. To. Bankroll. It."

Vic made a mental note to ask what that was all about later as Dani's GTO skidded to a stop in the parking lot.

A few days later, Dani danced around the dining room, humming as she set the table. Teddy Bear cocked his head and slogged off to the living room.

Is this really happening? She'd hoped Daddy would relent and let her play with the band, but it floored her when he approved Jon coming over for dinner. Suggested it, even.

No more sneaking around. Well, not with Jon, anyway. Still need to figure out how to tell him we're going on tour this summer. He won't like me putting college on hold. Lord, I know some things we sing in Inferno aren't pleasing to You. You must have arranged it, right? I mean, You brought Jon back to me, and he's reading the Bible and everything now. And Daddy even says it's Okay. Or that he'll allow it, anyhow. That's the same thing, right? Now, please, just help me talk him into—

As if on cue, Daddy wheeled in, looking like he was trying to suppress a grin.

Best mood he's been in since he's been home. Good a time as any.

"So, Daddy, there's this birthday coming up, and I was thinking… you know what would make a great present?"

"Think I can figure something out." He looked like the Cheshire Cat.

Dani cozied up to him. "There's these stage lights…"

He stiffened. She batted her eyelashes and put on her best seven-year-old grin, coaxing back his smile.

"They're really important, Daddy," she said, kissing him on the cheek.

"Your friend should be here any minute."

Vic looked at the office clock. He had twenty minutes before he needed to head out if he was to get a good seat to watch Dad grilling Jon for dinner. And he had a few questions of his own.

He looked back over the books a fifth time. Everything remained in order.

Picking up the phone, he realized he didn't know the number. He'd never needed to call it. He flipped through the Rolodex. 374-839-9221.

"Yeah?" Greg yawned on the other end. A kid giggled in the background.

"This is Victor Grassigli. Wanted to talk to you about coming back to work for Fidelis."

"Love to help Gunny out, but what I'm doing... I need the money. Your old man was more than fair, but let's face it, there was nowhere to move up there."

"Can you keep something quiet a few days? I mean, don't even tell my dad."

Vic waited a long minute. Silence.

"Listen, Dad's planning a big birthday party for Dani and me, and I'm waiting until after to tell him, but I'm planning to step away. I'm supposed to be a missionary, and I think it's time to pursue that. But they're going to need some help here. I've run the numbers, and I know we can beat what you're making once I'm off the payroll."

"Think Gunny's gonna be okay with this?"

Vic's turn to let a question hang.

"If Gunny and Dani need the help, I'm in."

Vic stared long and hard at the phone after hanging up.

One more call to make. Been twelve days. Can't keep putting it off.

ani set the last of the plates and moved to answer the door. Daddy beat her there, inspecting Jon like one of his Marines. It was the first time Dani saw Jon look scared. She walked behind Daddy, resting her hands lightly on his shoulders. Without averting his glare, Daddy grunted and wheeled aside for Jon to squeeze in.

Dani wanted to kiss Jon. Knew he could use it. Leaned in to hug him instead. On cue, Teddy Bear ambled over and squeezed between them. Dani scratched his ears. Shrugging, Jon followed suit, jerking his hand back as the dog let out a throaty growl.

"He doesn't bite." *Doesn't usually growl, either.* At Dani's rebuke, the dog plodded into the dining room, glancing back over his shoulder every few steps.

Within minutes, Vic arrived, and everyone seated themselves. Teddy Bear returned and lounged, one eye open, on top of Dani and Jon's feet.

Jon broke the silence. "Looking forward to church tomorrow."

Dani expected a response from Vic, but he just pushed his food around his plate. Dad narrowed his eyes like he always did when he was letting someone talk enough to dig themselves a hole. She reached for Jon's hand under the table. A yawn and a stretch from below and she got a handful of Chow Chow fur instead. Teddy Bear nuzzled into her, resting his mane on her lap. *Those aren't his table scraps eyes.*

"Any plans for a real job?" Daddy kept a low, matter-of-fact tone.

"Dad!" Vic pulled himself from his fog. "C'mon…"

Dani looked at the floor, ruffling Teddy Bear's head and reaching across for Jon's hand, overruling the dog's objection. *Daddy never grills Vic's girlfriends like this.*

"Fair question," Jon said, squeezing her hand and meeting Daddy's stare. "Little strange to lead with, though."

Silence hung in the room as they locked eyes.

"To be honest, sir, I do have a plan."

Daddy reclined, one eyebrow raised a squinch.

Please, please really have one.

"Giving the band one more year."

A year? Even Basil won't say we'll make it big that quick.

"I know lots of bands don't make it. And if we don't, I've always wanted to join the Marines."

ani shook her head as she cleared the table. She'd hardly got a word in, and now Vic had taken off, and Jon sat in the study with Daddy. Daddy had never been one for chitchat, but if there were three things that could get him talking, it was Christ, classic cars, and the Corps. And Jon had hit all three during dinner.

"Liked it better when Daddy hated him," she muttered, heading out to the back-porch swing.

Teddy Bear followed, plopping by the doorway and cocking an ear back toward the house. When Jon finally opened the back door an hour later, the dog rose and blocked him. When Daddy called him, Teddy Bear lumbered into the house, stopping to growl until Dad gave a firmer, "Sergeant Major Teddy Bear!" The dog always knew he was in trouble when Daddy called him by his full name and rank.

Daddy looked on approvingly as Jon made his way over to Dani, her feet up on the swing, sweater pulled around her knees. She pulled her hand back into the sleeve when Jon reached for it.

Confusion registered on his face. "You mad at me?"

She played with her nails.

"Thought you wanted him to like me?" He leaned in to kiss her, lips glancing off her cheek as she turned aside.

Wish you'd go away.

"I've never gone through all this for a girl. This is crazy."

"So don't." She felt herself biting her lip. Hard. Didn't care.

"Look, if we're going to go together—"

"I don't date Marines."

"That what's bothering you?" He laughed. Looking back toward the house, he lowered his voice. "Even if we weren't going on tour, I couldn't get in the Marine Corps. I dropped out of high school."

She hadn't known that. And while it did mean there was no way he was getting into the Marines, she still wasn't crazy about it. "You could always go back. Night school or something."

"Rock star, baby—no GED required. But wait, you saying you wouldn't stick with me if I went in the Marines?"

"Spent half my life living with my grandparents on a farm in Iowa and the other half wherever Daddy was stationed. Never stayed anywhere long. Don't want that life."

Chapter Fourteen

Monday, April 1, 1991

Dani's ears were still ringing from the midday underground concert Jon took her to.

"What was that?" she said.

"The future of rock 'n roll."

Dani rolled her eyes. "Thought that was supposed to be us."

"We've got five years to make our mark," Jon said. "Tops."

"You can't really think this stuff will catch on?"

"Wave of the future," Jon said, donning shades as he slid into his Fiero.

"It's punk repackaged, except they can't play or sing. And that look. Seriously? Lumberjack chic?"

"Dunno," he said, leaning over the stick shift to kiss her. "You'd look hot in flannel."

She half gagged, half giggled as she cranked the radio. "Ah, real music. Nothing good ever came out of Seattle."

Dani spent the next half hour with her bare feet on the dash, hair blowing in the wind, holding Jon's hand and thinking about how amazing her life had become. Sure, they'd both had to fib a little, but Daddy approved of their relationship. Vic seemed to be okay with it since Jon had gone to the altar and prayed to receive Christ last Sunday. Daddy was even trying to be supportive of her music. She wasn't so sure she'd convinced him it wasn't bad, and she knew he'd have a conniption if he knew she'd skipped school today to go to a concert, but you only turn eighteen once, right?

Not the first time I've done something like that lately. But what Daddy doesn't know won't hurt me.

"This isn't the way home," she said as Jon took a rural exit.

Jon smirked, pulling into a remote lot, shielded from the road by a stand of pines. "Thought we'd hang out here a while."

"If we're not to the party on time…"

"What'll they do? Take your presents back?"

He kissed her deeply, taking her breath away.

"Maybe a few minutes." She snuggled into him. "But our lights must have cost him a fortune. Least I can do is be on time for my own party."

"We can be quick."

"C'mon, no touching there." She moved his hand back to her knee. "We talked about this."

"You're eighteen now." He pulled back, sighing at the roof. "Not Daddy's little girl."

That stung, but she reached for him.

"Remember what Kari said?" She held up her hand, waggling her fingers. She hadn't taken the silver "Love Waits" band off since Kari gave them out. "Besides, why are you asking for a present on my birthday?"

"I stopped smoking. Quit pot. Haven't had a drink in a month. Just saying." A red tint crept into his face, and it sounded like he fought to keep his tone down. "What do you expect me to do, marry you first?"

Vic looked at his watch for the thousandth time. Friends, clients, the church family, everybody who was anybody to him and his sister would start showing up over the next couple hours. The Callahan grandparents were coming in from Iowa. Dad had even talked about inviting his brothers and sisters, but Vic was pretty sure he'd decided against it. Vic only remembered seeing them once, at Grandma Grassigli's funeral. He didn't remember much about the only time he'd seen his grandmother other than baby Dani's wails echoing through the Bronx cathedral.

Dad had asked him repeatedly over the last few weeks whether Dani was ready to take a bigger role in the business. Vic had done his best to give his answers a positive spin. *Hope the questions have something to do with her birthday present. Nothing could fit my plans better than Dad giving the business over to her. Lord knows, she's the one who likes it. And she got all the talent for it.* He checked his watch again. *Not going to help if she's late. Again.*

"C'mon, let's get this over with," he muttered. He had enough on his mind, figuring out how to tell everyone he'd taken the preliminary steps toward going on the mission field. *Thailand! Imagine that. Probably best I broke it off with Julie first.* He felt terrible for only trying to call her once since that night. He scolded himself for thinking he could lead her to Christ by dating her. *Seemed to work for Dani, though. And I really do like her.* He shook his head. "I'll call her tomorrow." He'd been telling himself that for more than two weeks.

"Hey, you!"

Vic jumped in his chair. *Figures Kari would be the first one here.* He made his best attempt at a warm smile while she glanced around the shop, all teeth when she realized they were alone. She sat beside him, closer than he'd have liked, playing footsie and making small talk until other guests mercifully started arriving half an hour later.

Within an hour, Dad was there, the grands were there, half the church was there, the shop buzzed with wall-to-wall conversation. Still no Dani.

Dad had been grinning nonstop for a week. No doubt, he'd planned for this party to be a big deal. It was unlikely anyone else could tell, but Vic saw from across the room that Dad was quickly losing any sense of humor he might have about her absence.

ani rolled down her window to give Jon one more kiss. As they parted, she tapped her watch.

"An hour, got it." Jon's tone suggested he was trying to pretend he wasn't still frustrated over what didn't happen on the side of the road.

Dani checked the time, let a word she'd never used slip, jumped in her GTO, and floored it. She smiled into the rearview as Jon jumped back, gravel pelting his jeans. *Hope he brushes his hair. Grands are gonna be there.*

She wished they could go together, but that would raise too many questions. As is, she would have to write another school excuse note with Daddy's signature. *Last one, hopefully. School's out in two and a half months.*

She pushed the speed limit as much as she dared. *Last thing I need is to get pulled over.* Local cops had figured out the road leading from the Starks' place, where she and Jon had met that morning, offered plentiful opportunities to bust drivers under the influence as they came and went from Inferno's rehearsals and impromptu shows. She smiled, knowing Jon had quit that stuff for her. He'd even taken to performing with a tequila bottle filled with water after Basil complained he was hurting the band's image. But the crowds who came to hear Inferno jam still drank. And smoked pot. And used who knows what else. And got pulled over. All the time.

Quicker if I take the back road.

Dani took the corner sharp onto the gravel road. She was going to be late. No helping that. But if she sped up a little more, she could keep it to fashionably late.

I can talk my way out of fashionably late.

Pop!

Dani clutched the steering wheel for dear life as the car fishtailed.

By now, Vic was almost happy to have Kari sitting beside him. If nothing else, the constant chattering gave him something to think about other than Dani being late again. Her friends had shown up almost an hour ago—Shelly, the rest of the church youth group, most of whose names he didn't know, even Jon arrived a few minutes ago.

Just like her to be late and not bother saying anything.

Vic hurt for Dad, knowing Dani's irresponsibility ate at him as he forced a smile and mingled with the crowd.

"So, what do you think?" Kari touched his arm for the hundredth time. Vic tried to remember what she'd been talking about. Came up blank. Shrugged.

"Yeah, I know," she said. "I just don't know if…"

Whatever Kari said next faded into the background noise as Vic watched Dad wheel up to Jon. With Dad's back to him, Vic couldn't tell if he was reading him the riot act, but Jon kept shifting his weight, shoulders hunched and eyes low, occasionally darting to the window. By the look of it, Jon was either explaining himself or that he didn't know why Dani was late, either.

Well, why would he? She should've come straight from school.

Whatever they'd said, Jon didn't stay long. *Was that worry on his face as he hit the door, checking his watch?* Vic made a mental note to clue Jon in about Dani's tardiness habit. *Guy will worry himself sick if he expects Dani to be on time.* He decided next time he talked to Jon, he'd apologize for how direct Dad can be. *I don't want him dating Dani either, but…*

"You think he's really saved?" Kari said, earrings flopping. "I mean, he still plays in that band."

"I think we need to be careful not to drown baby Christians." His tone was harsher than he'd intended. Seeing her jerk back, he softened it. "Give God time to deal with his heart. Dani seems to think it's real."

Not even going to mention Dani's playing in the band now.

Her look suggested she wasn't impressed with Dani's discernment, but she let the matter drop as Shelly dropped into the seat on the other side of her, sipping a bottle of 7-Up. She looked pale as she put her head on Kari's shoulder.

ani woke with a start. Head splitting. Tried to focus. Fluorescent blur. Two-headed Julie, rocking back and forth in her crisp police uniform, service caps tucked under each of her left arms.

Dani blinked until Julie was down to a single head and tried to sit up. Back came the second head and a third. Someone on the other side of her put a hand on Dani's shoulder and told her to lay back, asking if she was in pain as she poked, prodded, and took vitals.

"Just my head," Dani lied, looking at Julie. "Got a mirror?"

Julie looked surprised at the request but pulled a small compact from her pocket.

Dani flipped it open. Groaned.

"Nothing that won't heal," Julie said. "Car's not so lucky. I need to stop running into you Grassiglis on the side of the road."

As if on cue, Vic wheeled Daddy into the tiny room, flanked by Kari, Shelly, and Grandpa and Grandma Callahan.

Julie's jaw flexed when Kari let out a light gasp and put her arm around Vic's waist, but the expression was fleeting.

"Looks like my work is done here," Julie said. "Full report will be at the station if you want to see it." Julie put a warm hand on Dani's shoulder and looked up at Vic. "Take care of yourself. And happy birthday."

The nurse shooed everyone but Daddy out, directing them to the waiting room.

"Doctor will be around soon. If they decide to keep her overnight, you can visit after that."

"If?" Vic asked on his way out.

"Busy night," the nurse said. "Early tests suggest she's okay. Unless she's showing trauma, he'll probably send her home."

As Dani faded back into sleep, she felt Daddy's rough hand envelope hers.

Vic shuffled as fast as he dared down the hospital hallways, drawing disapproving stares from a doctor and a pair of nurses along the way.

Can't leave the grands in the waiting room long by themselves, but I've got to figure out which way she went.

By the time it occurred to him he'd have a better shot of catching Julie by the exit or in the parking lot, he knew it was too late anyway. He'd have to wait and call her when she got off her shift—not for a couple more hours.

He knew he couldn't date her. *Definitely can't put myself in that kind of temptation again.* He knew he'd done the right thing fleeing temptation that night. *But I do care about her. Maybe even love her. No. That's crazy. She's not even a believer. No way I can let that happen. But she does deserve to hear that from me.* And whatever else happened, he didn't want Julie thinking there was anything between him and Kari. *Nothing outside of Kari's imagination, anyway.*

Dani woke to Jon holding her hand. Daddy, Vic, and everyone else who had come earlier sat wherever they could find a spot around the room. Everyone but Julie, anyway.

Someone had brought in an enormous birthday cake on a rolling dinner tray table. Eighteen pink and twenty-four blue candles topped it, unlit. Looked like carrot cake. Her favorite. Didn't look like she was going home tonight.

Daddy smiled when he noticed her awake. She tried to smile back, but her head throbbed. Not quite as bad as before, but enough to make her grimace.

"I don't want to spend my birthday here."

"Doc said you're probably okay," Jon said. "But they want to keep you overnight just in case."

"We can celebrate tomorrow," Daddy said. "Or the next day. Whenever you're up to it."

"No, I'll be all right."

Daddy looked at Vic, who nodded and looked around the room. Dani thought he even looked approvingly at Jon. His brow furrowed as he looked at the cake. Jon, seeming to sense what bothered him, fished a lighter out of his jeans. Daddy inhaled sharply but didn't say anything as he lit the candles.

Dani smiled wanly as they sang "Happy Birthday." Kari sang the "Happy Birthday; God Bless You" version they always sang in youth group while everyone else sang the normal words. *Jon, do you really have to put on the rock star voice? I mean, it's "Happy Birthday."*

Vic covered any slack her bruises caused as the two blew out the candles.

Dani slumped back. "My car…"

Daddy hushed her. "Another day. You made it out, no small thanks to Julie."

Kari's smile faded a pinch, but she immediately pushed it back into chipper mode, cutting cake and serving.

As they finished up, Daddy sat straighter, speaking up as much as he could without drawing the nurse's ire. "I'd hoped to make a big deal of this and announce your presents in front of everyone, but…"

Jon's face lit up. Dani smiled, sure she'd hinted just enough.

"There are several smaller gifts for each of you back at the shop, of course, but I don't want to hold off telling you about your big gift."

Dani squeezed Jon's hand, stifling a squeal.

Daddy produced two stacks of legal-looking papers.

What?

"I'm giving you each a third of the company."

Dani felt Jon's hand go limp in hers.

"You've proven you can run it, even without me. And I've always dreamed of passing it on. I'll split my remaining third evenly between the two of you in a few years when I retire, and it'll be your business to run, with the provision that you need to keep it in the family. But for now, you'll be full partners. You'll have as much say as I do in all things and equal ownership of all property. Includes all the rolling stock—except my Trans Am, of course."

Daddy rolled over and brushed tears from her cheek with the back of his hand, smiling wider than she'd ever seen.

"Figured you'd be happy, but speechless and in tears? Knew in my gut this was the right—"

"How could you?" Dani brushed away the rest of her tears, feeling her face flush. "Daddy, really? I don't want your company. You think I want to spend the rest of my life in some smelly old garage?"

She regretted it even as she said it. Hated herself for the hurt she knew she was chiseling onto a face that never showed pain. But she couldn't stop. "I'm a musician, Dad! A musician!"

"That's enough."

She could tell he was fighting to control his tone.

Vic stood, speechless.

Figures. He'd take Daddy's side, anyway.

"I told you what I wanted—lights, equipment, stuff we need. For the band!"

Kari spoke up. "The first commandment with promise…"

"Who in the world asked you?" Dani retreated into herself, flaring back at her father. "I'm not a little girl anymore! Why can't I just have my half in cash so I can follow my own dreams?"

The door burst open. A ham-faced nurse. When she spoke, it registered just above a whisper. May as well have thundered. "Everyone. Out. Now."

Dani swung her legs over the side of the bed.

"Not. You." If Ham-Face's voice didn't convey business, her eyes sure did.

ani's room was cleared. Her head wasn't. She stewed. *How could Daddy think I'd want that? And I can't even sell it? How are we supposed to go on tour now? How dare they treat me like I'm still a little kid. Who does he think he is, making decisions for me?*

She wished Jon was here, but the nurse had kicked everyone out and sent them home, declaring visiting hours over. No matter what the sign said.

When Ham-Face returned an hour later, Dani met her with the question, "Do I really have to stay here?"

"Doctor wants to make sure you're not having problems, no concussion or anything."

Dani let the nurse continue her checks. Everything looked okay, but the nurse said the doctor preferred twenty-four hours under observation.

"Can I go?"

"You really should stay."

The door had barely closed behind the nurse when Dani reached over for the hospital phone.

A sleepy voice answered.

"Come get me. I'm an adult. I'll sign myself out."

Chapter Fifteen

The roar of butterfly wings in her stomach made Dani forget her lingering headache. She and Jon had been together on and off three months, but she'd never been in his trailer. Now, she stood at the door, looking in.

Jon had already flopped onto the foldout couch and was busy clearing old cans and piles of wadded notebook paper—songs that didn't make the cut, Dani guessed. The place reeked of sweat and stale beer. Two and a half slices of yesterday's pizza sat in an open box on the end table.

Dani swept away the crumbs of heaven-knows-what and slumped onto the other side of the couch.

Jon tried to make light, but Dani wasn't in the mood for jokes and said as much. He moved closer to her. She scooted away.

Seeing his face fall, she said, "You know I love you."

"Yeah, I know. Just don't want to be touched right now."

For once, he almost seemed to understand. No challenge. No attempt to keep pushing it. He just sat there, looking into her eyes until she felt like she could ignore the mess surrounding her and just melt into him.

He gets it. He knows I'm not just a kid.

After what seemed like forever, Jon rose and snaked his way through the piles of equipment and junk to the minifridge at the end of the trailer. Reaching into the tiny freezer partition, he returned with a green bottle.

"Know you don't do this," he said, sloshing the dark liquid in the half-full bottle.

"You don't anymore, either." Dani bit her lip. "You promised."

"Haven't had a drop in weeks," Jon said, setting the bottle between them. "Honest. It's Bobby's."

"Won't that make him…?"

Jon grinned, an exaggerated nod.

She had to admit, ticking Bobby off sweetened the deal.

"Trust me," he said, unscrewing the cap. "You'll feel better."

She picked the bottle up, looked inside, grimaced.

"Just once won't kill you."

She held the bottle high. "Here's to Daddy and Victor and Kari and everyone else who thinks I'm still just a baby."

"Slow down, babe, that ain't Pepsi," Jon said, grabbing the bottle as she sputtered.

"Ugh, what is that stuff?" She read the label—Jägermeister. "Tastes like black jellybeans."

Jon took a pull and handed it back.

She shook her head. "Grossest thing I've ever put in my mouth."

But two minutes later, she had to admit she did feel a little better. Light-headed. Almost giddy. And two swigs later, cradled in Jon's arms, she felt a lot better.

Chapter Sixteen

The first hint that morning approached showed on the horizon. Dani, blurry-eyed, slumped into the passenger seat of Shelly's mom's Oldsmobile station wagon outside Jon's trailer. Shelly had dashed for the bushes, bent over, and hurled as soon as she'd parked.

The sound made Dani's head pound. She felt like she needed to puke herself, her mouth dry, prickly.

Oh man, what if I'm...

She hadn't considered that possibility last night. And yet, even that idea didn't sting like knowing what she'd thrown away.

She felt hollow.

The white wedding, Mom's dress, that first night when she, with a new name and a new golden band, would hold her husband's hand, look him deep in the eye and, in some special, romantic place with new satin sheets, offer him the gift she'd been saving for a lifetime as they started their new life.

Until death do you part.

Lost. On the couch next to yesterday's pizza.

She laid her head on the dash and sobbed, glad Jon wasn't here to see. He slept like a baby when she'd pried herself from under him. Didn't notice her tears. Didn't stir when she'd called Shelly and begged her to come get her at three in the morning.

I'll never have that to offer ever again.

The words from Kari's purity sermon pounded in her head: *"I can be like you anytime, but you can never again be like me."*

The fading moonlight glinted off the purity ring. Dani took it off. Considered throwing it out the window. Fingered the etching: True Love Waits.

She slipped it into her pocket.

The driver's side door groaned, and Shelly flopped in. Dani couldn't remember seeing Shelly without makeup. Ever. The bags under her eyes had bags. Her pajama sleeve had caught some of the vomit. So had her tangled hair.

"You look terrible," Shelly croaked, reaching for Dani's hand. "Want to talk about it?"

"Just get me home. I need to get ready for school."

Twenty minutes later, Dani dragged herself up the porch steps and leaned her head on the front door before opening it as quietly as she could. She shushed Teddy Bear as he rose to greet her and wobbled through the living room on tiptoe. Stumbled. Stopped. Her bedroom door was open, and a voice projected from it—Daddy.

She hadn't considered the possibility Daddy would be awake so early. Or that maybe, like her, he hadn't slept at all. She eased herself onto the couch as Teddy Bear yawned and ambled over to her, and Daddy prayed in his strong, calm voice, reminding her of years of bedtime prayers. He prayed she'd recover quickly and be okay. Prayed for wisdom as a father, that he'd know what to do and how to guide his adult children.

And then Daddy prayed for Jon and the other members of the band.

He knows their names?

Daddy circled back, prayed forever about every imaginable aspect of her life. Prayed God would help her stay focused on Jesus, help her stay pure.

Teddy Bear nuzzled into her as she stifled a sob. She tried to shush him. He took that as his cue to hop on the couch.

"Shhhhh!" Dani said as the couch creaked.

The praying stopped.

Dani winced as the living room lights came on.

"You're home?"

Dani had rehearsed this, even if she hadn't planned on playing her part so soon. "Signed myself out." *Slow down. Don't slur.* "Shelly drove me home."

She felt like she was under inspection. Daddy controlled his facial expressions, but the veins on his neck popped and he couldn't keep the red streak from creeping up to his ears.

He knows. Everything. He can't. He can never know.

Dani tried to be coy, gave him her best Daddy's girl smile. "Knew you wouldn't let me just come home." She batted her eyelashes. Realized how silly that must look with mascara running down her cheeks.

Daddy's eyes narrowed slightly as Teddy Bear looked back and forth between them. She straightened to her full height, trying not to wobble.

"I'm not a little girl." She felt like a little girl. She continued rapid-fire to keep from slurring. "I'm-an-adult-graduate-in-two-months-work-hard-I-can-make-my-own-decisions. And another thing, I'm—"

"Right."

Dani stopped cold, cocked her head.

Daddy swallowed hard, stroking gray stubble. She'd never seen him with stubble. Or gray. He repeated himself, barely above a whisper. Even so, his voice broke, only the second time she'd ever seen him cry.

Later that morning, Vic sat slack-jawed across the desk from his father. "You can't be serious?"

Dad spoke slowly between slurps of coffee. "Mind's made up."

He looked like he hadn't slept in a week.

Vic let it all sink in. He knew the books inside and out. Giving Dani that much cash would clear him out. Even keeping the business operating would be dicey.

"Might mean running it ourselves when she graduates." Dad droned on about how things would go forward, his tone matter-of-fact.

Vic weighed asking him to just sell the whole company. *Let Dani chase whatever crazy ideas she has if he doesn't have the heart to do the right thing and tell her no, but at least give me my half, too.* A generous offer from Ed Wilkins waited in Vic's desk. He hadn't taken it seriously at the time. Hadn't even told Dad about it. But half of it would be enough to keep him on the mission field for a decade. He wouldn't even need to itinerate.

Dad tried to keep the pained look off his face. Dumb as it was to give in to her, Vic knew it had to be killing him to see Dani wasting her brains and talent on this half-baked rock 'n roll band. He glanced at the Missionary Society material laying on top in his open file cabinet. Worlds of possibility.

Setting his jaw, Vic closed the drawer. Laid his head in his hands. Shut his eyes. Massaged his temples.

"I need some time to pray about all this."

"I'll never do that again." Dani huddled in the quietest corner of the cafeteria with Shelly. Shelly's makeup was perfect, her hair flawless, spritzed to add eight inches to her height. Dani, still wearing yesterday's jeans, had barely managed to run a brush through hers this morning.

"You'll have a hard time keeping him if you don't."

Can't lose him. Not now.

"Alcohol," Dani said. "I meant alcohol."

"Everyone says that the first time. Did you get in trouble?"

"My dad acted like he didn't even know." She knew better. She knew it was silly, but Dani couldn't help feeling like the whole crowd milling around knew. Like the whole world looked at her differently.

Like they're not all doing it. At least, to hear them tell it.

She looked at herself differently. Closing her eyes, she tried to pretend it hadn't happened. Couldn't.

"I'm not going to lose Jon." She fingered the purity ring, still in her pocket. "Maybe too late for the whole love waits thing, but I can still keep myself to one true love."

Whatever it takes.

"Doesn't always work that way." Shelly dabbed tears.

A thousand needles poked at Dani's cheeks. "Bobby said he'd call."

"Guys say lots of things."

That night, Vic stood in the middle of the sidewalk wearing a baseball cap pulled low. He never wore hats. He spent way too long looking back and forth from the establishment's door to their sign. Hooligan's Pub. The marquee advertised live bands every weekend and fifty cent drafts on weeknights. He jingled the change in his pocket. *Wonder if a draft is different from other beers? Or is it even beer?*

People started to crowd the sidewalk, brushing past. A few walked into the bar. Not wanting anyone to recognize him standing outside, he hunched his shoulders and walked in, finding a table in the corner furthest from the door.

The place was empty except for a small group at the far end of the bar, all men with close-cropped hair. *Military, maybe? Nah, some of them are too old for that.* Whatever they were, they were yucking it up, swapping stories and slaps on the back.

"Cheeseburger," Vic said before the shapely waitress could get to him. He'd heard bars have the best burgers. "And a draft."

"Bud? Mick?"

Who?

"Corona?"

He'd seen that on a T-shirt once. "Whatever they're having," he said, nodding toward the backslappers.

Two hours later, he hadn't moved. He'd decided to leave twice, glad he hadn't seen anyone who might recognize him, then the door opened, and Julie stepped in and waved to the backslappers, who had added half a dozen to their crowd since Vic had been watching. That settled it. He motioned to the waitress subtly, hoping to pay his tab and get out.

Too late. Julie saw.

If Dani could have dissolved into the floor, she would have. She couldn't believe he'd do that. The first thing Jon said, in front of the whole band, when he saw her at rehearsal:

"How's it feel to be a woman?"

He smiled like it was no big deal.

Have I become an inside joke?

Dani strapped on her guitar, eager to avoid conversation. Cal averted his eyes as she struggled through the most basic chord changes.

"Can we try to get it right, princess?" Bobby was a six-pack in when Dani had arrived. He'd turned into liquid mouth.

Dani bit her lip, eyes on the floor. She felt heat creep up the back of her neck into her cheeks, knew they were morphing from embarrassed pink to deep fury red.

Bobby rolled his eyes, throwing an exaggerated whisper Jon's direction. "That's why we don't fool around with the help."

"That's enough." Jon stepped between them, finger thrust in his best friend's face.

"Basil's gonna be here any minute. Want him hearing us play like this?" Bobby pushed Jon's hand away, glaring at the others. "Somebody please tell him groupies are for after the show."

Dani couldn't make eye contact with him. She let her guitar hang from its strap and dropped her eyes, balling her fists.

Bobby shut up.

"Wasn't for her, you wouldn't even be in the show," Cal said.

Marc hit a rimshot-splash combo in an ill-advised attempt to lighten the mood.

Jon would later claim the only reason he hadn't hit Bobby was because Tom Basil arrived.

Before the door slammed, Basil started talking. "Wish you had that equipment I've been telling you to buy. You'll never believe who I could be booking you with right now."

"Told you, there's no way we can come up with that kind of money," Jon said, slumping against the amps.

"Actually…" Dani bit her lip, thanking God for the change of subject as she pulled the folded check Daddy had given her from her jeans pocket.

Basil did a double take, eyes as big as compact discs.

"Couldn't believe it myself," Dani said.

"It's a start," Basil said. "Sure it won't bounce?"

Julie waved off the backslappers directing her to an empty stool and walked over to Vic. He turned his attention to his draft. *Never did find out what kind of beer is in my glass. Is there really a difference?*

"How many have you had?" Julie said, concern in her voice.

I must look guilty.

She slipped into the seat next to him.

"Still on his first," the waitress said, behind her.

"Couple of root beers," Julie said, reaching over and taking a bite of his untouched burger. She came as close to making a face as she ever did. "How long's this been sitting here?"

"Sorry I didn't call."

She shrugged. Raised her shoulders half an inch, anyway.

"Bible says to flee temptation." He slumped, pushing the beer away as the waitress set the root beers down.

"That what I am?" A hint of a smile teased the corners of her lips.

Is that sadness in her eyes or just poor lighting?

"Also says not to be unequally yoked."

"Unequally what?"

"Means I can't marry someone who isn't saved. I'm going to be a missionary."

"Wasn't hearing wedding bells. And I didn't realize I needed saving."

"We all do."

She sat back, nursing the root beer and taking another bite of his cold burger. "They make the best burgers here. Better hot, though."

Vic made eye contact, looking as long and deep as he had on her balcony. "We've all sinned."

She smiled, nodded, motioned the waitress, ordered fries.

She's clearly not taking me seriously. At all. Still, have to try to sow seed. Maybe someday, she'll look back on it.

"Because we've all sinned, all done things we shouldn't and failed to do things we should, we all deserve justice," he began, matching the beginning of Pastor Stenger's weekly altar call word-for-word. "God's justice for unrepented sin is eternal punishment. In hell."

"Sounds harsh."

"To us, yes," Vic admitted. "Because we're not holy. We're not just. We don't usually compare ourselves with what's right and true. We compare ourselves with other sinners, like two prisoners arguing about whose crimes are less serious. Do criminals usually think their sentence is fair?"

She tilted her head.

Acceding the point?

"But God still loves us." He drained half his root beer. "So much He sent his Son Jesus to die on a cross to pay for our sins. We did the crime. He took the punishment. That's ultimate love. I mean, the Bible says that some might be willing to die for a good person, but God loves us so much that Christ died for us even when we were sinners."

The waitress set the fries down, hovering close by.

"He calls us to repent—to turn around—and just believe that He paid the price for our sin, that He wants to save us. That He wants us to spend eternity with Him in heaven. All He wants is our heart."

She finished the burger and wiped at her chin. "Sign me up."

"Me, too," the waitress said.

He felt like his head was on a swivel, looking between the two. "Just like that?" He'd had people respond to altar calls when he'd preached, but this was the first time he'd ever led someone to Christ one-on-one.

"Isn't that what you said?" Julie said. "It's in the Bible, right?"

He picked his jaw off the floor and nodded.

"I believe," Julie said, her voice and expression as deadpan as ever. "Jesus wants to save me. I've sinned. I need it. I want to be saved."

"Me, too, if he can forgive me," the waitress said, wiping tears.

Vic stuttered his way through leading them both in a simple prayer, admitting they had sinned, acknowledging their need for a savior, confessing they believed that Jesus died for them and that God had raised Him from the dead, and that they wanted Him to save them and to rule in their hearts and lives.

"Amen," they repeated.

The waitress, still dabbing her eyes, wandered off to help other customers, leaving Vic to stare at his new convert in stunned silence.

Finally, he said, "You know what this means?"

"If you and the preacher are right, that I'm going to heaven."

"No. Well, yeah, that. But," Vic said, taking her hand, "this means we can date now. I mean, we still probably shouldn't be in your apartment alone, but we can have a relationship."

"The yoked thing?"

He nodded vigorously.

"Jesus seems like a no-brainer," she said, pulling her hand back. "You, I'm going to need to take some time to think about."

Chapter Seventeen

It didn't hit Dani just how much money Daddy had given her until she opened her own checking account. The teller got the supervisor, who got the manager, who got someone in a three-piece suit, who called her dad to verify the check was legitimate.

Within a week, she had a checkbook, a purse full of credit cards and a spending limit beyond anything she'd thought possible.

The band would get everything they needed—lights, better amps, sound equipment, everything top of the line. It amazed her how much stuff her bandmates didn't know they needed until she had money to pay for it.

Oh well, not like it's going to clean me out. There'll be plenty left for me and Jon to start a life after I graduate, even if the band doesn't make it big.

She had no idea what a house cost but was sure she had more than enough.

That Saturday, Basil loaded the band into his Cadillac and headed south to LA. Dani sat in Jon's lap in the back seat looking out the window, not bothering to make him watch his hands. *Not like it's a secret.* They hadn't been alone since her birthday, but she knew it was just a matter of time.

"Best costume designer in LA," Basil said. "Works with all the big names. We're lucky to get in on short notice."

Up front in the passenger seat, Bobby popped in a demo cassette. Lone guitar, simple riff. Basil nodded and tapped the beat on the steering wheel as Bobby's thin voice came over the speakers:

*"Give me a ticket for the fornication station
The night is still young, and I'm way behind..."*

The rest of the lyrics made Dani blush, embarrassed even to listen to it in a carful of guys.

After listening through the song twice, Basil grunted. "Chorus works, riff's good. I'll fix the verses. Dani sings this one."

"I'm not singing that."

"Dani already sings two songs in our set," Jon cut in. "What am I supposed to do while she's in the spotlight?"

"I'm not singing that," Dani repeated, her voice lost in the mix as everyone spoke over each other.

"Shake a tambourine or something," Basil hollered, glaring at Jon in the rearview mirror. "Heck, have Bobby teach you the three chords he knows, and you can play along."

"C'mon, quit ragging on Bobby," Marc said. "He's not that bad."

Dani and Cal voiced agreement.

"Forget it," Bobby said, punching the eject button. "It's my song. She's not—"

"Not singing it," Dani singsonged above the jabber. "I will not sing it here or there. I will not sing it anywhere."

That silenced things for all of three seconds.

"You saying something's wrong with my song?"

"Trust me," Basil said once things settled down. "Dani sings this one, I'll get it on the radio."

"My dad would kill me."

"He already paid for the video," Basil said, the car swerving dangerously close to the center line as he argued into the mirror. "Besides, he's a stump-jumper. Not like he's coming to an Inferno show, and they sure aren't going to play it on the gospel channel."

Dani hung her head. He wasn't wrong. Daddy had agreed to let her make her own decisions, but she knew he didn't approve of Inferno's brand of music. No way he'd come to a concert, not even to see her.

Fornication station, huh? She beat back a tinge of shame. *Train's already left that destination. Not like playing in a band is the worst thing I've done lately.*

reg was waiting at the shop when Vic and Dad arrived. He offered to help his old sergeant out of the truck, but backed up, hands high, and smiled when Dad glared at him. In a matter of minutes, the trio stood inside over what was left of Dani's GTO.

"You'd think she could buy her own now," Vic said. "Easier to replace it. Cheaper."

Dad didn't seem to hear as he did slow laps around the wreck.

Greg popped the hood and made a face. "Ain't unfixable."

"Come on," Vic said. "Money it'd take to get this back on the road— it's not worth it."

Dad set both hands on the twisted bumper. "We're fixing it."

"Maybe it's not as bad as it looks," Greg offered.

"It's every bit as bad," Dad said.

Vic shook his head. "As a partner, I have to say, this isn't good use of—"

"So, Dani's playing in a band now?" Greg stepped between the two.

Vic narrowed his eyes. *He's needling me.*

"Dani's got a good head on her shoulders," Greg said, checking the motor mounts. "How bad can it be?"

What Dani are you talking about?

"You don't know the half of it," Vic said.

"Bet you haven't even seen her show."

Vic turned his back, pretending to focus on the car.

Why'd I hire this guy back, anyway?

Dad's voice was barely audible from under the hood, but his words were final. "We're fixing this."

❝I'm not wearing this," Dani called out. Inside the dressing room, she looked in the full-length mirror. The outfit, mostly red lace, covered her most private parts. Barely.

"C'mon, let's see it," Basil said, all but Cal chirping agreement.

"One of us already has." Marc laughed.

Dani stiffened. Checked the door. Locked. *Good.*

"I'm not wearing this."

I look like a stripper.

She reached for her stonewashed jeans and T-shirt as the guys outside argued in hushed tones.

"It's just a costume, Dani," Jon said as she slipped the T-shirt over her head. "It's just us. Don't be such a—"

"Fine." She tossed the shirt aside and opened the door. Hands on hips. Weight on one foot. Glaring. *Where's Cal?* She bit her lip hard to stop tears as the rest of the band, and Basil, whooped and hollered. Retreated. Shut the door.

"That one," she heard Basil telling the designer as she dressed. "And one just like it in black—but cut it closer. How soon can we get 'em? Just booked our biggest show yet."

Dani felt like a hooker.

❝No time for this. Got stuff on my mind." Vic shooed Teddy Bear, but Dani's dog wasn't having it. He'd get up, do a couple of "idiot laps," as Dad always called them, and curl back around Vic's feet. Worse, every so often, he would stare, wait for Vic to make eye contact, and emit a low, whiny growl, almost a whimper. Vic tried letting him outside. The dog looked at him like he was nuts.

The dog finally plodded off into Dani's room after Vic tripped over him on his way to answer the phone.

Julie.

"Just listen." Her voice was steady as ever. "Sorry if I was hard on you. A missionary, though? That's heavy stuff."

"Being a cop isn't?"

Vic moved the receiver away from his ear, looking at it in response to a solid buzzing sound. "Got another call. Hold on a sec."

Kari.

"Look, I'm going to talk to Dani, but I wanted to talk to you first. I know she's been playing in that band and you know why that's not okay. I have to tell her it's either them or us. She can't play in the praise band if—"

Promising to call her back, Vic clicked back to Julie.

"Look, I'm not even sure I'll be able to go on the mission field," Vic said. "With Dani chasing this stupid band thing, I'm going to be stuck here helping Dad. Maybe for a long time. Someone has to."

"Sorry you're stuck there," Julie said. "I know how that feels. Kind of what I called to tell you. Didn't want you to hear it from—"

"Hold on a sec, got another call coming in."

"Again?"

Shelly.

"Dani's not here. Try Jon's."

"I always know where Dani is." Shelly spoke in hushed tones, faster than she usually talked. "Listen, I'm calling because I don't know who else—"

"I have a call on the other line. Can I call you back?"

"You've got to get her away from those guys."

The usually giddy, giggly Shelly was sniffling. Vic forgot about the other line.

"Listen, he's going around telling everyone."

Who's telling what?

Vic decided to leave the question unasked, not sure he wanted the answer.

"I'm so sorry," Shelly sobbed openly. "I didn't know, or I never would have introduced her to those guys. Listen, if anyone can tell her, you can, but you can't tell her I told you."

"Told me what?"

"He's seeing other girls."

Vic sighed. Relief. That might actually be good news. If he was going around bragging about two-timing Dani, she'd put a stop to that. Fast. Vic shuddered, almost feeling sorry for Jon.

He ended the conversation and clicked back to Julie. Nothing. Tried calling her back. No answer. *Guess I'll try later.*

Back in street clothes, Dani imagined her face was still as red as the glorified teddy Basil wanted her to perform in. She bit back tears.

No way I'm going to let them see me cry.

Taking deep breaths, she put her foot down. "I'm not—"

"Listen," Basil's tone was soft but firm. "You want to sell records? You want to fill seats? Show 'em a little leg."

As if leg is all that getup shows.

"Jon, you can't possibly be okay with the whole world seeing me like that?"

"We're a rock band," Jon said, lighting a cigarette—something else he'd told her he'd quit. "Ain't gonna kill you."

"That's settled, then," Basil said. "Now we just need—"

"She said she don't want to wear it." Bobby jumped in with a stream of expletives. "Look at her. She's ready to cry."

Cal looked at Bobby sideways, but he and Marc fell in behind him, calling on Basil to ease up.

"We're a good band," Bobby continued. "She don't want to play half-naked, she shouldn't have to."

Slumping, Jon stammered, "Can't she wear something else? Not like she's the singer."

Basil shook his head but relented. Two more hours of trying things on and arguing back and forth later, they finally picked out a pair of stage outfits he'd approve that Dani could live with. They showed more than she would have liked, but at least they didn't make her feel like something out of a girlie magazine.

Long as Daddy never sees me in them. He'd die.

Next, it was the Ryder brothers' turn to find outfits. Sitting in the lobby with Bobby and Marc, Dani thanked Bobby for speaking up.

He waved her off. "We both know why I'm still here. And you don't have to tell me again. I know I need to call Shelly and work something out."

Her look must have asked the question for her.

"I don't know. Soon."

"Pay phone's outside."

Before he could object, she slapped a handful of change on the end table between them.

D ad's voice echoed off the shop walls, startling Vic awake. He rounded up the missionary brochures he'd scattered over his desk.

"Please!" Dad prayed.

He must not realize I'm still here. Vic could count the times he'd heard his father raise his voice on one hand. Now, his voice had all the fervor of a Marine barking orders on the beachhead.

"Guard Dani. Protect her. Protect her friends."

Vic silently prayed along. *Who knows? Dani could turn around.*

"God, I'm afraid I've made a mistake."

Not your fault. Vic considered letting Dad know he was there until sobs echoed off the shop walls. *Gonna be hard on him if Dani crashes and burns.*

"Lord, I feel helpless here, and I don't know what to do with that. I've done my best to steer my kids in the right ways, especially since I've known You. There has to be something I can do other than watch as they turn their backs on what I've built for them."

Vic looked at the brochures one last time before laying them as quietly as he could in the wastepaper basket.

Chapter Eighteen

Dani hadn't seen Shelly since she'd dropped out and started going to night school almost a month ago. Easier with the morning sickness, she'd said at the time. She looked good. Except for the start of a baby bump stretching her teal sundress, she looked as put together as ever. The two found a seat inside the town's only McDonald's.

"Why aren't you answering Bobby's calls?"

"Hello to you, too."

"Been busy." With Inferno's first arena show coming up, it wasn't a lie. "We kill at this show, we could be opening for Cinderella's next tour. We get that and…" She patted Shelly's tummy. "Little Bobby'll be set."

Shelly looked like she was trying not to make a face. "You talked to Vic?"

"Every day of my life," Dani said between chicken nuggets. It wasn't like Shelly to hold back, and there were never any secrets between them. "What kind of question is that?"

Shelly looked down into her strawberry shake. She dipped her fries in and ate in silence for a long minute. "I don't want Bobby around the baby."

The shock must have shown on Dani's face.

"I love Bobby," she said, laying a protective hand over her bump. "Or, I thought I did. But I don't want him around doing coke and who knows what else."

"I'm around those guys all the time. He smells like weed sometimes, but…"

Shelly's eyes shut her down.

"Jon too?"

Shelly looked at the floor and nodded.

No. Dani balled her fists under the table. *He quit. He's not even drinking anymore since that night. Promised he was done. Said I was his drug of choice now.* "I can't lose him."

"Maybe God has someone better?"

"What are you, Kari now?"

"Been talking to her a lot. She says it's always better to do things God's way, even if it costs something now."

Dani lowered her voice to a whisper. "I don't want to be that girl who slept with lots of guys."

Shelly looked like she'd been slapped but composed herself quickly. "You don't keep a guy that way anyway."

"What would you know about that?" Dani regretted it before she even let it fly.

Shelly pushed herself from the table, face reddening as other customers looked on. "You're a real one-man woman?"

Dani reached for her friend. "I'm sorry. I didn't mean—"

"He's not a one-woman man."

"Liar!" *Who cares who's looking?* "There's no way he would—I don't need to listen to this. Just because you couldn't hold on to Bobby doesn't mean—"

The color ran from Shelly's face as Dani turned on her heel. Shelly's voice trailed behind, softer now. "Why would I lie?"

Dani tried to slam the door. The hydraulic hinge swooshed. She let out a primal groan and stomped off. *It's one thing when Daddy and Vic trash Jon, but Shelly?*

"Just be careful," Shelly called after her.

Dani threw a gesture over her shoulder she'd never used before.

The next morning, Vic finally saw his opportunity. He'd had something to say to Dani for a couple weeks, but she was always with Dad. Or, worse, with Jon and the rest of that bunch. Now, she sat in the corner, lost in her Cap'n Crunch. In an hour, she'd be on the road, off to Inferno's big show.

Not if I have anything to say about it.

He positioned himself so she'd have to push through if she wanted out. "You grew up singing in church."

She looked at him, shoulders slumped.

No fight?

Vic softened his tone. "Aretha Franklin. Whitney Houston. That guy in Guns 'N Roses. Know what they had in common?"

She shrugged, pushing the bowl away, half-full of soggy corn cereal.

"Grew up singing in church. Every one of them."

"They did okay." She sounded half asleep.

"God gave them a gift, and instead of using it for His glory, they sold themselves to the highest bidder. For what? A few dollars more?"

"A few?" Dani rolled her eyes. "Look, I don't want to talk about this."

"Dani, you can't keep playing that music." He slammed his hand on the table, making the spoon rattle in her bowl. Her back stiffened. *Finally.* "You have a gift. Don't flush it down the toilet for—"

"You think I'm doing this for money?"

"What else?"

"You know I don't need money. You wrote the check."

"You can't seriously tell me you're doing this for…"

"I love him."

"Then tell him he shouldn't be singing those kinds of songs, either."

She stood, looking like she was deciding whether to push through. Flopping back down, she said, "It's not that easy."

"You don't stop hanging around those people, you're going to wind up doing things you regret."

She grabbed her bowl and started shoveling, refusing to look him in the eye.

A chill cut to the base of his spine. He started to ask. Sputtered. Couldn't stand to know. He had one bullet left. She could come back, work for Dad. Maybe in six months, he could revisit the missionary society. "Jon's seeing other girls."

"Why's everyone trying to break us up?" Before he could blink, Dani stood in his face. "Jon's a lot of things, but I've got him wrapped around my little finger. I made him wait a long time. He's never waited that long bef..."

Shock registered on her face.

Vic stepped back, trying to clear his head.

The waterworks came on. "You can't say anything. Please!" Dani buried her head in his shirt, stifling a scream. Shook. Dabbed her eyes. "I've got a show to do."

He watched her until the door closed. In a haze, he washed her bowl and spoon and put them away.

Chapter Nineteen

Basil walked onto the stage area as Dani and the rest of the band finished their preshow checks.

"See the sound guy?" He pointed to a gangly dude who looked like he'd missed the memo that he was getting too old to rock 'n roll. "Go talk to him."

"About what?" Dani nuzzled into Jon while the rhythm section headed to the dressing rooms.

"Who cares? Just talk sweet."

Dani hesitated.

"We nail this show, it means big stuff. And that guy," Basil said, pointing again, "decides whether to crank it up or put us at half power like every other opening act. Flirt with him a little."

Dani looked over at Jon, who shrugged. "It's only rock 'n roll, Babe. Don't mean nothing. We need to kill it tonight."

"Can't believe you're okay with this," Dani said, storming up the stadium steps toward the sound booth. *Can't let him down.*

Gangly seemed to notice her about halfway up, openly leering.

All he's missing is some drool on his chin.

Dani leaned over the sound booth's half-wall, well out of earshot of the stage area. She glared down at Basil and Jon as the sound man leaned back, lighting up and blowing smoke in her direction.

"Help you?"

She painted on her sweetest smile. "Listen, we both know why I'm here."

"We're sorry, you have reached a number that has been disconnected or is no longer in service. If you feel you have reached this recording in error, please check the number and try your call again."

Vic did. Same recording. He fished his quarter and nickel from the coin return. *Great. One more person to worry about.*

Hands in pockets, he shuffled toward home, the sunshine on his face threatening to lighten his mood. *Love California in the late spring.* Changing his mind, he turned on his heel, putting the sun to his back and cutting through the patch of shade trees in the park. *Shop's closer. I'll just use one of the cars there.*

Twenty minutes put him at the shop, surprised to find Dad had already left. Two more minutes saw him behind the wheel of a Chevy Nova that was scheduled for a transformation from drab green with rust patches to Royal Plum sometime next week.

With no FM on the dial and no AM Christian stations in the area, he rode the fifteen minutes in silence, arguing with himself whether he should even be going there with what happened last time.

But he needed to talk.

There was no answer at the apartment door. He knocked louder. Again, louder still.

The next door over opened, revealing a neighbor with female pattern baldness and a cat under each arm.

"Looking for the weird cop?" She said, an unlit cigarette flopping. "She's gone. Took a job with the LAPD. Moved out last week."

Vic found a pay phone outside the apartment's office. Wasn't the best place to make a call, with kids splashing in the nearby pool, but it's what was there. Plugging his outside ear, he asked for Los Angeles directory assistance. "Julie Porter, please?" He spelled it, groaning under his breath when he realized he didn't have anything to write the number down.

"Sir, we have no listing for a Julie Porter in Los Angeles. Is there another listing you'd like to try?"

He hung up and started to walk away as the sun found the only cloud in the sky to hide behind.

He turned back, muttering to himself as he dialed the phone, "Any port in a storm."

It only rang once.

*D*eep in the bowels of the Cow Palace outside San Francisco, Dani hung her stage outfit on the doorknob and searched for a mirror amid stacks of long-forgotten boxes in what passed for a lady's dressing room. A half-dozen brand-new banners of teal sharks eating hockey sticks were the only things in the room not covered with a thin layer of grime and dust. At least it had a shower—more of a mop closet, really.

She found the mirrors behind the sharks with the odd diet and ran a finger through the grime, revealing her reflection. The air conditioning had gone out in the band's van during the drive, and she felt sticky.

She removed a stack of old concert posters from the room's only chair. The one on top looked like the band Jon had taken her to see on her birthday. The poster billed them as Nirvana, saying they'd played the venue in December. *How in the world did those guys get to headline anything?* She used the posters to wipe enough of a clear spot on the mirror to do her hair and makeup.

She debated whether she could get by without a shower, pretty sure she'd seen spiderwebs in the stall. No one would be close enough to smell, and she'd need another after the show anyway.

The door creaked. Jon, smiling wider than ever.

"You're not supposed to be in here."

"See the crowd?" He made his way through the piles. "Sixteen thousand!"

"C'mon, it's gross in here," she objected as he embraced her.

In the end, that didn't matter.

Rather die than disappoint him.

Kari set her glasses on the picnic table, dabbing running mascara for the hundredth time and holding Vic's hand the whole time he poured out his guts.

"I'm scared for her." Vic heaved. He'd stopped trying to hold his own tears in hours ago. "And for Dad. I'm glad he doesn't know the half of it."

"All you can do is pray," Kari said, squinting. "Wait for her to come around."

"I've failed. This started on my watch."

She pulled his head to her shoulder, stroking his hair. "Love never fails."

Dani wrapped herself in a towel and stepped out of the mop-closet shower. According to the clock on the wall, she had forty minutes for hair and makeup. *Like I'm going to trust the clock. Fool me once.* She reached for her watch.

It was gone. Along with the pile of clothes she'd left on the floor and the stage outfit she'd left hanging outside the shower.

"Jon, this isn't funny!"

But this wasn't something Jon would pull. He'd had his fun. By now, he was probably telling Bobby all about it.

Who then? Who would dare? She fumed, too mad to be scared. Then she saw it.

The red lace outfit hung from the doorknob.

"Lots of kids get off track for a while," Kari said.

Vic wondered if that was supposed to be comforting.

"I mean, look at Shelly. She…"

"Got knocked…"

"Where there's sin, there's even more grace."

"She's still pregnant."

"Is that the end of the world?" Kari held him at arm's length, her face a mess of tear-streaked makeup. "Dani's not out of reach."

"You haven't seen how bad it is."

"Need the room. Time to get out," the stage manager bellowed from the other side of the door.

"I can't wear this!"

"Come out in the buff for all I care. Need the room for Mad Hornet's guitar player. Singer won't share a room with him."

They were higher on the card.

"Where am I supposed to get ready?"

"Don't care."

Dani wanted to scream. "Give me five minutes." The glorified negligee wasn't much, but it was better than her birthday suit.

"Two. And you wasted one of 'em arguing."

Three minutes later, Dani shivered in the hallway, trying to ignore the catcalls of every passing stagehand while she worked frantically on her hair and makeup in a compact mirror. *No way I'm going to be ready.*

Basil called from behind. "Time to go."

She turned, wishing she could knock that silly newsboy cap off his head as he looked her up and down. Who did he think he was? Brian Johnson?

"You look hot, but ain't you gonna brush your hair or something?"

She threw the compact at him. Big mistake. It shattered, leaving her without any type of mirror. She pointed at her outfit. "This is not—"

"Forget it." He whipped his cap off and plopped it on her. "Nobody'll be looking at your hair anyway."

ani stared out at the sea of faces crowded into Cow Palace, feeling like she needed to throw up. Seemed like a lot more than the sixteen thousand Jon said were out there. The crowd was raucous when she was waiting backstage. When she stepped out, they turned it up to eleven.

Wish I had more than my guitar to hide behind.

But when she hit her first chord, everything faded but the song. She could strangle Basil later. She could be self-conscious Dani Grassigli later. Tonight, she was Dani Glass, and she had a show to do.

Inferno broke into Dani's version of "Mind in the Gutter." Jon had argued against opening with it, but Basil insisted. The song was getting local airplay in San Fran and would be the only original on their setlist anyone in the crowd would recognize.

From the first note, Inferno had all the volume they needed and then some. Dani couldn't believe how easily Old Gangly had agreed to change the settings. *Maybe not as big a deal as I thought. Maybe they're right, and I just need to loosen up.*

The more the crowd responded, the more Dani threw herself into the performance. The more Dani threw herself into the performance, the less inhibited she became. Strutting along the stage front, she forgot her near nakedness and reveled in the fingertips reaching out for her, too far to touch, but close enough to feel the energy. She hadn't touched a drop of alcohol since *that* night, but feeding off the crowd's screams produced the same electric feeling as she locked in tight with Cal and Marc. Even Bobby was dialed in.

The stadium roared as she looked straight into the eyes of the crowd and cooed the final lyrics:

"Come on, who wants to get a little dirty with me?"

She spotted Stoner from school in the front row. Conscience raked her guts, knowing she was inciting him and everyone like him in the crowd to lust, as Kari would put it, but she didn't have time for embarrassment. Shoved it down. Turned her backside to the crowd as they erupted.

And then Jon stepped to the mic.

Shouting, screaming, whistling, all fizzled to a dull murmur. By the end of the second song, she wondered if she heard a boo. By the middle of the third song, she didn't have to wonder.

"Let the chick sing!" someone yelled.

"Yeah, bring back the..." The terms quickly became crasser.

Halfway into the set, Dani dodged a bottle. Kept playing. Something hit Cal. He stopped, cussed no one in particular, and found his place back in the song. Marc got the worst of it, much less mobile behind his drum set than the rest of the band. She couldn't see Jon's face. Didn't need to. Even from across the stage, she could see the muscles in his neck and back tense, and there was no mistaking his rage as he screamed the lyrics.

In the wings, security and the stage manager flailed their arms.

Are they calling us to get off stage?

Bobby put a hand over his mic and leaned toward her. "We can't go off like this." Before Jon could launch into another song, Bobby hit a power chord and shouted, "Got one we been working on. Gonna give the mic back to Dani Glass!"

"Get on board before we leave you behind,
Come with me and let me blow your mind..."

By the time she reached the chorus, Inferno had the crowd back in their corner.

"Get a one-way ticket for the fornication station..."

Dani leaned into the audience as she launched into the solo. Hands raised toward her as the spotlight morphed the faces into a sea of dots. Security forcibly persuaded one fan not to join her on stage. The spotlight shifted. *Is that? Can't be.* Dani saw a familiar face in the third row. *Kari?* She was fighting the crowd. Dani's shame surrendered to red-hot anger. *Can't sing that next verse with her here. Never be able to show my face in church again. Can't not sing it.*

As the last notes of the song faded out and the band met at the front of the stage to take a bow, Dani's eyes settled on a man in the crowd. How he got a wheelchair that close, she'd never know. She'd seen every imaginable look on his face over the years, but she'd never seen Daddy look like that. She dropped her guitar and ran backstage.

Chapter Twenty

Dani blindly careening off amps, crates, stagehands, and anything else in her way. Vic. Yelling. She bowled him over. Gangly Sound Guy grabbing her. *Am I ready to what?* Vic knocked the cigarette out of Gangly's mouth. Crashing. Fight. Security!

Found a corner. Rocking. Head between knees.

"Daddy!"

She screamed.

No.

"I'm sorry!"

Can't go home. Ever.

She heard herself sob. Sounded like someone else. Everything spinning. Band laughing. Jon yelling.

Basil's claw on her bare shoulder. "Dani's Inferno. Get it? Like Dante…" Cackling.

Jon yelling. At her. "I'm the lead singer. You can't name my band after…"

Cal: "Santana."

Marc: "Fleetwood Mac."

Bobby: "Van-freaking-Halen."

"Shut up!" Dani screamed.

Blinded. Swinging. Throwing.

Arms pinned.

"Take this," Basil said.

A pill in her mouth.

Chapter Twenty-One

Tuesday, July 2, 1991

V**ic turned off the TV. Someone in that band got arrested. Again. It was getting so that it was hardly news. Still, it was the only way he knew his sister was alive. He turned it back on to see if he could get a glimpse of her, but the announcer had moved on to other celebrity news. Some real estate mogul from New York proposing to an actress Vic had never heard of—Marla something-or-other.

He went out to check the porch. Sure enough, Dad had fallen asleep in his wheelchair again. He spent most of his time lately staring down the long driveway. Three days' worth of stubble graced his chin.

Vic wheeled his father to his room, careful not to wake him as he parked the chair and covered him with an afghan. Sometime in the middle of the night, Dad would wake enough to pull himself into bed. Probably.

At least it gives me another day until I have to tell him how shaky the business has become. With the wages Dad insisted he pay Greg and the two new employees he'd had to hire to fill the void Dani left, Vic doubted he could keep it afloat much longer. Dad knew everything there was to know about restoring cars, but he had no idea how big a hit it would cause when he gave half of the company—the liquid half—to that ungrateful brat.

Vic was afraid to ask, but part of him still believed Dad had only intended to call Dani's bluff on the whole music thing. He'd figured—and he thought Dad did, too—that Dani would be back in the shop, a few dollars poorer and a lot wiser, in a matter of days, weeks at most.

147

Dumb idea even if it had worked.

Sitting in his own bed, Vic reached for his Bible on the nightstand and opened to Galatians. Two verses in, he set it back down. *Too tired. I'll read extra tomorrow.*

Dani flopped on the couch in the penthouse flat she and Jon shared, her mind racing, head throbbing. The latest Pioneer 100-CD changer played some thrash band Jon liked on repeat. Where the remote disappeared to was anyone's guess.

The sleeping pills weren't working anymore.

When she'd insisted they find a real apartment after two days of living in Jon's trailer, she didn't have dropping out of school and moving to LA in mind. She didn't have sharing the three-bedroom flat with the rest of the band in mind. She definitely didn't have the $3,900 per month rent in mind. She'd spent the first couple weeks expecting her father to come looking for her.

Her life had become a blur. Nights playing the Sunset Strip ran into days hanging out fliers up and down Sunset Boulevard and Rodeo Drive. Twice, she'd stayed out past dark hanging the advertisements. Both times she'd been mistaken for a prostitute and propositioned.

She took another pill from the unmarked bottle. *Basil said these things would knock me out. Basil's an idiot.*

She thought about picking things up. The squalor was almost as bad as it had been in the trailer, though Jon had filled the place with pricier toys. A plasma screen TV the size of a small zip code, KISS and Rolling Stones pinball machines, box on top of box of electronic gadgets Jon hadn't even bothered to open after bringing them home in his new Corvette.

Dani had no idea how much money she had left, especially after dropping $60,000 on the new video for "Hit the Door Runnin'." Basil had wanted the band to do the video on "Mind in the Gutter" or "Fornication Station," but Dani refused to do the things the producers wanted for the video concepts. When Jon dug in his heels and insisted the first video release should feature the lead vocalist singing, Dani backed him, and Basil quit fighting about it.

The video was seeing airplay and, on the strength of exposure on MTV, the song hovered just outside the Billboard Hot 200.

This place needs a dog. Hope Teddy Bear's all right.

The door opened, Jon backing in.

"Where you been?" She slurred.

Ignoring her, Jon called over his shoulder, "Clear a spot in the corner for it." Pulling the remote from his pocket, he turned the stereo volume down.

"What did that cost?" Dani said as a pair of uniformed delivery men grunted through the door. They carried an E-Mu Systems Emulator III, according to the box.

"Fourteen."

"Hundred?!"

"Thousand. You should see what this thing will do."

While the delivery men set the keyboard up on an accompanying rack system in the corner, Jon repeated what the salesman must have told him about all its bells and whistles.

"You don't even play keys," Dani said.

Chapter Twenty-Two

"You can't just give up," Kari said, both of Vic's hands in hers. "She's your sister."

"Even if I knew where she was, I'd be arrested for trying to talk to her. I can see the headlines now. So much for any kind of ministry then."

"Dani didn't file the restraining order. Their manager did. You just need to catch her away from the rest of the band."

"Good luck with that," Vic said, fighting back tears. "But you don't know what she did to Dad. I don't even know what I'd say to her if I did see her."

"Well, you could start with—"

"This is dumb. I would try, but I don't even know where she is."

Kari smiled. "Maybe God will make a way."

Two days later, Kari pulled her yellow Yugo into the Fidelis parking lot as Vic headed out for lunch.

"Hop in. We'll get something to eat."

He didn't have the energy to argue. *If I'm not careful, she'll ride my lethargy all the way to the altar.* He shot her a where-to look as she buzzed past both of Rio Flaco's restaurants. She looked like she was doing her best to suppress a grin as she looked back at him over her glasses.

Fifteen minutes later, she turned the nose on to 395 South.

"I can't be gone—"

"Worked out. Greg assured me he could handle it."

"No."

"C'mon, you wouldn't go to the fireworks last night." Her mascara threatened to start running.

Vic slumped in the seat. "Where are we going?"

"Out to eat."

𝕯ani crushed her cigarette before greeting Shelly.

"You're huge!" *Probably not the best opener.*

Shelly laughed it off as the two embraced.

"Ooh," Dani said, feeling unexpected movement. "Is that?"

Shelly nodded. "If you sing to them, they'll dance."

"They?"

"That's what the doctor says."

"You'll love this place—real LA classic," Dani said as she led the way into Carney's, a restaurant inside a renovated yellow train car.

It was quiet for a Friday, maybe a little early for the dinner rush.

"Get me what you're having," Shelly said, picking out a window table in the back and taking the wall seat that faced the entrance.

Within minutes, Dani slid the platters of chili burgers and fries onto the table. "So, does Bobby know yet?"

Silence.

"He's trying." Dani felt weird defending him.

"Been getting the checks," Shelly acknowledged. "He still doing drugs?"

Dani's turn to be silent.

The two picked at their food, Shelly peering out the window every minute or so.

"Heard our song on the radio yet?"

"Been listening to the Christian station." Shelly checked her watch, putting a hand on her belly as she checked out the window again. "I want to do this right... right as I can, anyway."

The small talk continued until Shelly cut Dani off, mid-french fry. "I need to use the bathroom." Bracing herself against the table, she pushed up and waddled off.

Dani lit up another cigarette. She hadn't imagined Shelly's visit would stress her out, but something was off. Not way off, but just enough. *Maybe it's the hormones.*

"I'm starving."

The hairs on the back of Dani's neck stood on end at the familiar voice. *Vic.*

She took a deep, quick drag before looking over her shoulder. *Kari, too. Perfect.*

Shelly came out of the bathroom and sat at a different table across the restaurant, facing away as Kari tapped Vic on the shoulder and pointed.

Vic's face fell. Kari nodded at him, kissed his cheek, made that silly over-the-glasses-googly-eyed look at him, and slid into the chair opposite Shelly.

Dani pretended she hadn't seen Vic seeing her. She crushed out her cigarette, feeling like she'd been caught in the girls' room.

It took forever for Vic to walk the length of the rail car. He continued past her, leaning his head against the wall. Dani couldn't look at him.

"Say something," she said.

After a long minute, he faced her, leaning against the wall and running a hand through his hair.

"Please."

He started twice, turned red-faced, collected himself. When he managed to make words come out, they were barely above a whisper. "You know this is killing him?"

Dani felt her ears burning.

"You're all he can think about. Come home."

"Can't."

"He hasn't cut his hair since you left. It's over the collar."

Dani wept.

"What's gone is gone. Just bring whatever you have left and come back, full partner. I forgive—"

"Don't need anyone's forgiveness," Dani said, louder than she'd intended. She looked out the window as people started to stare, watching her brother's reflection. "Not yours, not even our father's."

"At least marry the guy if you're going to—"

"Don't need you telling me what to do. I'm not a little girl."

"Then stop acting like one! You know, you're leading him astray, too."

Dani re-lit her cigarette as he walked away, letting it burn in the ashtray as she buried her head in her hands. She couldn't make out the argument on the other side of the rail car, but the last thing she heard Vic say on the way out was, "I'm not hungry."

She fumbled through her purse, hands shaky. No luck. She'd left the pills at home.

"I'm sorry," Shelly whispered, behind her. "I thought—"

"Go away."

Kari waited until Vic opened her car door to speak. "I was just trying…" She must have seen by his look that he wasn't in the mood to talk about it.

"I'll find my own way back."

He was three blocks down the Sunset Strip when Shelly pulled her mom's Olds up next to him. "I'm sorry."

Vic blinked, pretending he hadn't been crying.

"It's my fault, you know."

He tried telling her it wasn't.

"I introduced her to all of it—metal, partying, the band, Jon."

He didn't want to talk about it. Said as much.

"Kari's right," Shelly said. "We just need to…"

Vic crossed in front of her car into Sunset Boulevard. He heard the squeak of her passenger window cranking as he picked his way through traffic.

"She's still your sister!"

He pretended she'd been drowned out as he crossed the median.

Standing outside her flat, Dani heard Basil's voice.

Great. Company.

She tried to slip in quietly and go directly to her room, hoping to avoid whatever they were arguing about.

"Telling you, could have landed that Skid Row tour if you'd listened to me."

Jon and Basil thumbed through rock and metal magazines as they talked, half a dozen lines of white powder on the glass tabletop between them.

I'll yell at him later.

With Dani's inheritance providing digs most up-and-coming bands could only dream of, Inferno's penthouse was quickly becoming known as the go-to place to party. She was surprised there weren't any strangers passed out on the floor now.

She wanted to curl up and die in her room, the only part of the flat that wasn't messier than Jon's old trailer. She inched her way along the wall.

"Second place to Pantera's not so bad," Jon said, opening the magazine to a picture of the Texas metal band.

"Third," Basil said. "Nirvana turned 'em down cold."

The grunge band? How'd we lose out to the flannel-wearing weirdos? She decided to worry about that another day.

"Ha!"

Dani jumped as Basil pointed at a picture buried toward the back of *Power Chord Metal Mag.* "There you are."

Even from across the room, Dani could see the photo clearly. Jon, backstage at The Tricks, three women in varying stages of undress clinging tighter than his spandex. She bit her lip, felt it drawing blood. *Just go to the room, Dani. Fight about it later.*

Jon snatched the magazine. Maybe it was his smirk. Maybe it was the way he laughed. Maybe it was the way he admired himself in the picture. Maybe it was the way he casually tossed it aside when he was done. Dani felt her temper turning up to eleven.

Later, she couldn't remember what she'd said, but she was sure her father wouldn't have approved of it. She vaguely remembered flipping the tabletop, spilling $500 worth of cocaine into the Berber carpet, Jon yelling, punching, Jon's bloody nose, Jon calling her names she wouldn't have even used on the girls in the photo.

Am I all those things?

Years later, she could still hear Basil's laugh.

A dozen tattered musicians shoved leaflets at Vic as he walked up and down Sunset Boulevard. Most of them littered the strip now, but he folded the one listing Inferno on the bottom of the ticket for tomorrow's show at the Whisky A Go Go and shoved it in his pocket. He'd never heard of the other bands, but that was no surprise. *Could be top of the charts, for all I know.*

He guessed he was an hour's walk from where he'd left Shelly and Kari when he turned around at the corner of Western. The palm trees looked black, backlit in burnt orange.

This is a different world. And my sister's alone in it.

And then night fell.

"It's just a picture." Jon had said it a thousand times.

Dani turned over.

"Still not talking to me?" She felt his hand on her shoulder. "You shouldn't have gone out today. You need to watch what you're spending. Basil said we might not have enough to finish the video for 'Den of Vipers.'"

She was glad he couldn't see the look she shot him as she threw the covers aside and stumbled into the living room. *Shouldn't have taken that third sleeping pill.* She couldn't get her mind off the image of Jon practically wearing those girls. She looked at the other bedroom doors, the doorknobs seeming to vibrate in the haze. *Not one of these guys would turn me down on Jon's account. Cal might.* She looked hard at Bobby's door, coughing a disgusted laugh. *That'd show Jon. And Shelly.*

She shook her head, curling up on the blue jean loveseat.

You're not that girl.

Within minutes, Jon was snoring. *Must not be too worried about me not talking to him.*

Vic picked up his pace as the side streets puked every spandex and spike-wearing drag queen rock star wannabe in creation onto Sunset. He jumped out of the way of a seven-foot-tall monster with studs and razors menacing from all corners of his outfit only to back into a pair of prostitutes in black leather.

Add a little fire, and I'll bet hell looks just like this.

He pushed his way through the pushers and pimps and the hookers and the bass players.

"Hey baby, need a friend?" The streetwalker had the darkest eyes he'd ever seen.

Who would know? I have the money. Why should I always be the one to do the right thing?

"Let me tell you about my best friend," he said.

"For $200, I'll make you forget your best friend, your girlfriend, and anyone else who might be on your mind."

"Jesus. Let me tell you about Jesus. I'm a Christian."

"Lots of my customers are Christians," she said, coming in for the kill.

Vic balked as a police cruiser drove by, sending the girl and dozens like her clamoring for the shadows.

Was that Julie in the passenger seat? Hope she didn't see me.

He hung his head and walked as fast as his feet would carry him.

"Place isn't fit for animals."

"Didn't you sleep?"

Dani shook her head. It was unusual for any of the guys to stir before sunrise, but Bobby? He never got up before noon.

He joined her on the balcony. "Bark's worse than his bite."

"You heard that?"

"Who didn't? But you gotta get some sleep. Big show tonight."

Dani needed no convincing. She'd never felt so exhausted. But even a fourth sleeping pill hadn't slowed the images racing through her brain. Jon with those other girls draped over him. The disappointed look on Vic's face. The way she'd shoved Shelly away. And Daddy. She'd done everything in her power to drive the image of Daddy's face at the Cow Palace out of her mind. She wanted to scream. She didn't have the energy.

"Try this," Bobby said, glancing over both shoulders and pulling something that looked like a tiny purple balloon out of his pocket. He poured white powder from it onto the table.

"You know I don't."

"It'll help you forget the fight." He set a short tube next to the drug.

"When Jon does it, he bounces off the walls."

"Nah, that's coke." Bobby chuckled, double checking over his shoulders. "This ain't that."

"Keep this up, and Shelly's never going to let you see your babies."

"Babies?" He shook his head, squinting into the sunrise and calling Shelly one of the names Jon had used for her the night before.

Dani smacked him.

Bobby laughed. "If you don't wanna forget…"

Dani snatched the tube.

Chapter Twenty-Three

D ani didn't care.

For the first time ever, she didn't care.

She'd thrown up, slept six hours, thrown up some more. She'd never felt so completely relaxed. Every problem she'd ever had was suddenly no big deal. Only one thing had ever made her feel anything close to this— the presence of God. This was like that, with her foot on the sustain pedal.

Feels like I am God.

Even the bickering in the background seemed distant.

Who cares, anyway?

She was floating.

"What did you give her?" Basil's face turned the prettiest shade of red.

"Give Ol' Paunchy Mullet some, too," Dani said. "He could use it."

"Blah, blah, blah," Basil kept carrying on about something.

"You're one to talk," Bobby said, "with the stuff you've been giving her."

Bobby laughed. Dani joined him, vaguely aware of herself trying to make Jon and Cal see what was funny. They didn't seem to get the joke. Jon looked mad. Dani giggled.

"We gotta be at the Whisky in an hour and a half for sound check." Jon sounded whiny, like Vic used to when she got to work late.

"Work?" She knew nobody else heard that part of the conversation going on in her head. Didn't care. "I don't work. I play. Let's play."

"No way she can play in that condition," Jon said, grabbing Bobby by the shirt.

"Just trying to make her feel better."

"We agreed," Jon said. "No—"

"Sleeping with the rentals," Bobby sang, laughing. "Don't blame you, though. I would, too."

Should punch him for saying that. Or maybe Jon should. Dani fell into a fit of laughter, not sure what was so funny as Jon growled something about before the show and after the drugs and "Dani never did it before."

Funniest thing he's said yet.

Dani dozed off, still laughing and wishing she could feel like this forever.

Dani's head buzzed as Inferno faced the packed house. Long days of posting fliers and long nights of partying paid off. People knew who they were—the latest hot band in a town that eats hot new bands for breakfast.

People were starting to come to see them specifically. A handful wore Inferno T-shirts.

As much as she hated to admit it, Basil was probably right. The mostly male crowds probably had something to do with her increasingly skimpy costumes.

She always hated that part of it. Tonight, she didn't care. From the first note, she performed with an abandon unlike anything she'd ever known. From her moves on stage to her finger work on the fretboard, Dani threw every ounce of inhibition to the wind. And the crowd at the Whisky pulled down the rafters.

The rest of the band packed up backstage while Dani searched for Jon. The headlining band's ear-splitting sound chased her into the alleyway.

She squinted. Jon. Wearing a pair of blondes.

Flashbulbs split the darkness.

Inhibitions flooded back. Nerves raw.

I feel naked.

Screaming. Smashing cameras.

As the hounds retreated, Dani spun toward Jon and his new friends. Two steps toward them and the girls took the hint.

"It's for an album cov—"

"Shut up!"

"It was all Basil's—"

Dani told him in no uncertain terms what he could do with their manager, spinning on her heels to head back into the Whisky.

Basil stood in the doorway, blocking her way and laughing. "You want to be rock stars or Ozzie and Harriet?"

"What's wrong with being Ozzy?" Jon said.

Dani shoved past Basil, sending him tumbling into a pair of trash cans. She turned back to Jon. "I can have any man in that place."

All it earned her was an eye roll.

"So do it."

"Maybe I will."

Waking alone in a strange motel the next morning, Dani remembered her threat vividly. She had no idea whether she'd made good on it.

Chapter Twenty-Four

Sunshine snuck through a bent slat on the Venetian blinds in Vic's room. *Must've forgot to set the alarm.* He looked over at the clock. Almost 6:30. He gave his armpits a sniff. *If I skip the shower, I'll have time for devotions, long as I make it quick.* He'd skipped the last two days.

His Bible wasn't on the end table where he usually set it. Come to think of it, he hadn't seen it since Friday morning, before Kari took him on that ill-conceived trip to Los Angeles.

She'd left messages on the answering machine yesterday expressing concern over not seeing him in church. *At least someone noticed. Dad didn't.*

"Should probably call her back today."

He rifled through his desk. Bible wasn't there, either. *Maybe I left it by the couch.* He stumbled into the living room.

He saw it.

The burgundy, genuine leather Thompson Chain-Reference Bible with his name in gilt script on the cover. His fifteenth birthday present, from back when $85 was a lot of money for the Grassigli family. A real preacher's Bible.

Chewed to shreds.

Pieces of India paper pages laid scattered across the floor, neon blue and yellow from highlighted passages giving it the look of confetti.

Vic sank to the floor.

Teddy Bear, laying outside Dani's door, opened one eye, cocked an ear, closed the eye.

Vic took three strides toward the dog, snatching the rolled newspaper from the coffee table. Teddy Bear gave his tail a wag and a flop, eyes still closed.

Vic tossed the paper back onto the table.

"Deal with you later."

𝕷 ater that morning, Vic shuffled through the piles on his desk, trying to decide which bills could wait. He moved the stack off his mother's Bible, dusting it off and leafing through it. *Too much to do right now.*

Greg flopped into a chair across from him.

"Don't you knock?"

Greg rapped three times on the desk. "Need a new detail man."

"We have a new detail—"

The main bay door slammed.

"Need a new, new detail man."

Tires squealed, and gravel pinged off the aluminum siding outside the office.

"I can't keep calling clients and telling them we're going to be late because Corporal Punishment keeps running off the help," Vic said.

"You rather tell 'em the job ain't gonna be done right? Don't think Gunny would like that."

"Dad's not running the company."

"Clearly. Look, I ain't saying you can't stay in here and keep shuffling papers. Just get me someone that can do the finish work like Dani. Better yet, get Dani back."

"I'll talk to her agent," Vic said, pulling a stack of résumés from the filing cabinet. "Meanwhile, that rusty white T-Bird needs to be Peacock Blue by Monday."

Greg stood to his full height. "You need to get Gunny back in here. All that sitting at home's not good for a man."

"Monday. You don't have time to tell me how to run the company."

Much as Vic hated to admit it, Greg was right. It would do Dad good to get his hands dirty. Besides, Dad could be on the job tomorrow. Hiring someone new would take days—if he was lucky. *Even if I find someone right away, there's no telling how long he'd last.* Dani wasn't coming back, but Dad had taught her everything she knew, and he was the next best option.

That decided, Vic turned his attention to returning phone calls before closing time. He tried Kari, but she wasn't home. *Not in the mood for that conversation, anyway.* He confirmed an appointment to fill in for a pastor taking a missions trip to Peru next month.

"Wish I was going with you."

As soon as Vic opened the front door that night, Teddy Bear bowled him over.

"Stupid dog!"

His blood boiled as he dusted himself off, dragging himself back into the mess he'd left behind this morning. There, in the pile of tattered Bible pages, sat a steaming pile.

"C'mon, Dad, you at least have to let the dog out," Vic said under his breath.

He considered calling Teddy Bear back into the house, since he'd clearly already taken care of business. *Forget it. The dog will find his way back when he's ready. Or he won't.*

"Going to beat him to within an inch of his life when he does come in," Vic muttered as he cleaned the mess. "Should just put him to sleep. What is he, like ten? That's got to be old enough."

Seemed like the dog's only purpose was to remind Dad that Dani was gone, anyway.

In the tatters, Vic found a full page ripped clean except for a bite mark in the bottom corner. Proverbs 12, Vic noted. He'd highlighted a couple verses in green.

"He that is despised, and hath a servant, is better than he that honoureth himself, and lacketh bread." Verse nine.

And "He that tilleth his land shall be satisfied with bread: but he that followeth vain persons is devoid of understanding." Verse eleven.

Vic glanced through the skylights. "You trying to talk to me about the business or Dani? I already prayed for her today."

Then he noticed the unmarked verse in the middle, in simple black and white:

"A righteous man regardeth the life of his beast: but the tender mercies of the wicked are cruel."

Teddy Bear let out a low whine and scratched at the back door.

Sighing, Vic slid the glass door, dropping to a knee and taking the dog's mane in his fists as he leaned in to eye level. "Hasn't been easy for you, either, has it?"

Teddy Bear licked him on the mouth, the taste of dog tongue making him sputter and jump back.

Stifling what he wanted to say, he tousled the dog's head. "Promise I'll spend more time with you. But why didn't Dad let you out?"

An hour later, having frantically driven every street in the neighborhood, Vic called the police. "He didn't take his car... he's in a wheelchair... last time I saw him? About seven in the... no, last night... Didn't want to wake him when I left... I don't know what he's wearing, probably a Marine Corps T-shirt."

Chapter Twenty-Five

"You can't be serious?" One glance at the cover and Dani tossed the newly minted cassette aside.

"How bad can it be?" Jon snatched it, turning and cussing Basil. "I told you not to change our name!"

"Dani's Inferno," Basil said. "Like Dante—"

"Who?" Jon said.

"Trust me. It'll sell records."

"Call it whatever you want," Dani said. "Just change the picture." If it had revealed any more of her, it would have been censored.

Basil admired the camera work on the cover. "Every fourteen-year-old boy in the country will buy it."

Dani's stomach churned. *How'd I become the exact thing Kari warns the boys at youth group to stay away from?* She did her best to push the image of teens leering at her picture out of her head.

"Who cares about the picture?" Jon said, ignoring her reaction. "It's nothing the whole world hasn't seen by now. But this is my band. How dare you change the name?"

"Dani's Inferno's the opening act for the Rock Gods Tour," Basil said, smirking. "How do you think I booked that? You're a good-looking kid, but let's face it, you're just another skinny blond singer. Besides, it's already on the posters that way."

Jon's face darkened when he turned the cassette over. "You cut 'Cold War?' And 'Mirror, Mirror?' I only sing on half of these."

"That too many?" Basil said.

Marc and Cal grabbed Jon before he could reach the promoter.

"Trust me, kid, I know what I'm doing."

Dani didn't have the energy to argue about track listings, even though a couple of the songs featured lyrics so objectionable she'd only agreed to sing them after Basil promised they'd never see the light of day. She couldn't get the image out of her head of church kids hiding her band's cassette so their parents wouldn't see her on the cover.

"You have any blow?" Dani whispered to Bobby as their bandmates restrained Jon. *Only thing I know that'll make that still, small voice shut up.*

❝What do you mean cleaned out?" Dani demanded in the tour bus that afternoon. "Of all people, I know you're not getting on my case for being stoned."

"Don't care what you snort but you gotta figure out a way to pay for it," Basil said. "You're broke. Busted."

Dani was surprised how easily profanity spewed from her. "We can't be through all of it?"

"Unless Bobby's got a stash—"

"The money, I mean."

Basil lit one cigarette off another. "Told you, you're down to zilch. Nada. Unless you want to rethink that spread for *Playboy*?"

Dani glared.

"Check's a check, kid." Basil stepped in closer, the smell of stale tobacco overpowering. "Besides, the exposure a centerfold brings will sell records. Look, I didn't tell you to start a habit. I did tell you to lose one, though, and you didn't listen. You could have afforded the drugs till the next advance. The video featuring Johnny Boy, not so much. Cost 120 large. Barely shows you and MTV tossed it in the circular file. When you people gonna realize I know what I'm talking about?"

"It's his band."

"We all know who the star is. So does he."

"I'd rather be his girlfriend than his guitar player."

Basil let it drop as the tour bus door opened and the rest of Inferno spilled in, cases of beer under each arm. Dani wrinkled her nose. *Hate beer. But if it's all we have...*

"I was thinking this next album, I'll just play guitar," Dani said, cozying up to Jon after a couple beers. "Maybe some BGVs."

"Talk like that, there won't be a second album," Basil snorted.

Dani ducked for cover as Jon hurled a can of Coors, narrowly missing Basil.

"Fifteen cities down," she mumbled, huddling behind the gear as the fight threatened to tear the bus apart. "Forty-five to go."

Things went downhill as the tour progressed into fall. Dani was sure Basil was holding out on her money but had no idea what to do about it. He kept her in just enough heroin to relax, just enough coke to make it through performances. A few times, she resorted to hanging out with the headliners when she was low and Basil didn't deliver. Her recollection of those nights was fuzzy.

Jon pushed her away more and more. He wanted her when he wanted her. Most of the time, he just yelled at her. She felt like she couldn't do anything right. *Is it my fault the sound guys crank the system when I play and turn it down to half for him?* She'd offered to stop singing, but her songs were the ones hanging just outside the charts. *Guess that's my fault, too.* Even if Basil hadn't insisted she keep singing, the label would.

Jon knew that.

Didn't stop him from blaming her.

ani stared at lines of cocaine on a mirror between her and Bobby backstage in, best she could remember, someplace in Texas. Vomit rose in her throat, but she managed to hold it down. *No more. Can't do this.* It wasn't so much the bad dreams or the night terrors that had become an everyday occurrence. It wasn't even the weird hallucinations she'd started having. At least, she thought they were probably hallucinations. Mostly. *Pretty sure those midgets that show up every once in a while and run around in the penthouse throwing makeup all over the place are the real deal. But who knows anymore? Who cares?*

Bobby didn't seem any more inclined to take a hit tonight than she was. Wasn't like him, but he seemed lost in thought as he slumped against the gear cases. Dani offered him a cigarette, but he waved her off.

"Shelly called."

"That's grea…" Dani said as his face fell. "What happened?"

"Babies were born. Boys."

"But they're okay? Shelly's okay?"

"They don't know. It was two months early, and they're not doing good."

"What are you doing here?" Dani felt herself start to shake.

"She won't let me see them anyway." Bobby balled his fists. "Not till I'm clean."

Back in the dressing rooms, Basil and Jon started arguing. Again. Something about the setlist. Dani did her best to tune it out, but it looked like it was getting under Bobby's skin.

"Haven't had any since yesterday morning." Bobby held his hand out so she could see it quiver. "No idea how I'm gonna play tonight."

"Thought about rehab?" Dani said.

"Can't quit the tour. Child support to pay." He grabbed the mirror and flung it like a Frisbee, white powder streaming to the floor like confetti as the glass shattered against the wall.

Marc walked past, stepping around boxes and crates.

Probably on his way to settle Jon and Basil down. Always the peacemaker.

Looking at the shards at his feet, Marc whistled. "Mirror say you ain't the fairest in the band?" He laughed at himself, looking Dani and Bobby up and down. "Tough crowd."

An hour later, Inferno played the toughest crowd they'd ever faced. Bobby played half a measure behind most of the night and Dani spent the whole performance on the brink of passing out. At one point, a beer bottle hit Cal in the head. She'd never heard him yell like that before.

Halfway through the set, Jon made a lewd gesture to the crowd, another toward the band, and stomped off stage.

It didn't improve much when Dani stepped to the mic. She forgot half the lyrics, couldn't get her fingering right, and, for the life of her, couldn't figure out why the stage was spinning.

For the first time since she'd joined the band, there was no encore.

"We're lucky we even got off the stage," Marc said.

"What was that?" was all Cal managed as Dani shook herself to keep the fog at bay.

The shaking brought waves of nausea. Dani knew she needed to sit, but she needed to find Jon more. *He's going to be furious but better to deal with it now than back on the bus.* She stumbled toward his dressing room, steadying herself against the wall with one hand, the other on her stomach.

Then she opened the door.

She wanted to scream. Wanted to cuss him out. Wanted to cuss her out, whoever she was.

She closed the door softly and walked away.

Fifteen minutes later, Jon found Dani rocking in the corner, head in her hands. She refused to look at him as he tried first to apologize, then to justify, then finally to blame her.

"Wouldn't have come to this if you didn't hog the spotlight all the time."

She glared at him. He hadn't bothered putting his shirt back on.

"Stand up and talk to me." He grabbed her wrist, pulling her up.

Dani balled her free fist, blinking hard as she tried to decide which of the quavering Jon faces to hit. She started to fight nausea again. Quit. Puked all over him. Sat back down. *Serves him right.* She was only vaguely aware of the filthy names he called her as she was blacking out.

When Dani woke, Basil stood over her while Cal and Marc fanned her.

"Tell Jon he's fired," she said weakly.

"About time," Basil muttered. "You sure?"

"He's out of Dani's Inferno. And evicted." Dani closed her eyes, hands on her stomach.

"You got the flu?" Basil said. "Knew something wasn't right."

No way I can tell him. Her voice a shade over a whisper, she asked, "Where's Bobby?"

"Hit Jon for yelling at you, then hit the nose candy," Basil said. "He's sleeping it off in his dressing room now."

He never woke up.

Chapter Twenty-Six

"September 3, 1970-August 30, 1991," Dani read on the memorial card. "Would've been his birthday today."

Over Basil's objections, she wore a modest black dress.

Shelly sat four rows back, Kari beside her. Dani left her bandmates and slipped to the other side of her friend. *Hope Daddy shows up. Or even Vic.* Inferno wasn't big enough for their rhythm guitarist's overdose to make national headlines, but she figured everyone in Rio Flaco had to know.

A robed priest mumbled a few words about Bobby Van Zie. Dani wondered if the clergyman had ever met him. One of Bobby's family members read a passage of Scripture, a few people offered up memories, mostly from his childhood, and the priest offered hope that Bobby was in a better place.

Dani doubted it.

Teddy Bear whined, trotting to the door and chasing his tail. Vic shushed him and peered out the window. A black limousine drove by at no more than ten miles per hour.

"I hope she stops, too." Vic followed the dog as the car drove past and his whine gave way to a low growl. "Whoa, boy. I can't make her. Wish I could."

"What's the sergeant major fussing about?" Dad wheeled into the room. "Police still out there looking for me?"

Vic shrugged as the taillights disappeared around the corner.

Chapter Twenty-Seven

Even after a month had passed, Dad wouldn't let Vic off the hook for calling the police on him. Nevertheless, he had settled nicely into his new role as an employee in the company he'd started. His disabilities slowed him a little, but he hadn't lost his touch. And with the country riding a new wave of patriotism, news that a disabled war hero was on staff was starting to draw a trickle of new clientele. Not enough by a long shot, but the light bill was paid.

And since Kari had stopped pushing him to call Dani, Vic's life was becoming downright livable.

"Just wanted to thank you for sending your friends our way," Vic said when he heard Mr. Wilkins' voice on the line. "Saved out bacon, really."

"Suspected things might be tight."

"We can always use more business."

"Quality's back up."

Vic bristled but forced it to stay out of his voice. "Dad's back. Helps."

"Girl hasn't quit on the music thing yet?"

Vic clenched and unclenched his fist. "You sending more business our way soon? Just trying to schedule things."

A long silence hung over the line.

"I'm done sending cars to you," Wilkins said, his voice steady, business-like. "And referrals."

"You can't be serious?" Vic's brain flooded with calculations.

"Been wanting to be in the business myself for years. Got my eye on a restoration shop I think I can own for the right price."

This will sink us. Not only did Mr. Wilkins and his friends represent a significant chunk of their business, but his connections among classic car collectors would undoubtedly draw customers away.

"Or I could buy Fidelis. I'll write you a check for $5 million today. You and the sarge will never have to work another day in your lives."

"That's generous."

"Includes rolling stock, of course. Especially the TA."

"You know I can't sell the Trans Am. There's only three more like it on the planet."

"Nonnegotiable."

"Not mine to sell. And you might as easily ask Dad to sell Dani."

Vic could hear Mr. Wilkins sucking his teeth. He watched the clock tick off two whole minutes before the businessman spoke again.

"Without the TA, I'll give you three and a quarter."

Now it was Vic's turn to be silent.

"I have other prospects if you're having trouble making up your mind."

The phone clicked. Vic listened to the dial tone a full thirty seconds before hanging up.

Vic spent the rest of the week mulling over the offer. He doubted Wilkins would act right away, but he had no doubt he'd be competing with him soon if he didn't sell.

He looked at the number he'd written on a legal pad for the thousandth time. Enough to make sure Dad retired in style. Not just the typical military retirement. *And I could spend the rest of my life on the missions field. I wouldn't even need to itinerate or worry about money. I'd never be able to work through half that much. I could probably give half of it away to other missionaries and still be all right.*

He pictured Kari strumming her guitar and leading singing in some exotic language in the rain forest of who-knows-where, their three American children—all girls—mixing it up with the native boys and girls at her feet. In a year, maybe two, they could be there. Except their American kids, of course. That would take a few years.

The phone rang. A vendor wanting to make sure they'd received their invoice. Vic assured him they had, explaining it was going to take at least a month before they could pay it. "Business has taken a bit of a bad turn."

He did his best to remain professional when the man called his character into question.

"C'mon, that's only a couple weeks later than we've always paid you."

The man threatened litigation if the payment wasn't made on time.

Vic leafed through his old Missionary Society brochures after hanging up. One call and a few days of letting Wilkins' paper shufflers hammer out the details with whatever hack lawyer he could afford, and this would be all over. He leaned back in his swivel chair, practically feeling the tropical breeze on his smiling face.

Out in the bay, Dad whistled the Marine Corps hymn while wrenching on the Studebaker Big Six Wilkins' friend had brought in.

Vic slumped. *Be able to get him the best care available. Live-in care, probably.* But Dad had just started showing signs of life again. The thought of strangers caring for him ate at Vic's insides. Sliding the brochures back into the desk drawer, he dialed Mr. Wilkins.

"Come to your senses?"

"Yes, sir." Vic sat ramrod straight. "Fidelis Restoration is not for sale. At any price."

Chapter Twenty-Eight

Dani stared out the tour bus window, the Japanese signs a neon blur. "Fornication Station" fell off the Billboard charts two months ago without cracking the top hundred, but it was climbing at number thirty-six here. What was left of Inferno would soon face a sold-out crowd at Mielparque Hall in Hiroshima. Last show of the tour.

"Strike while the iron's hot," Basil said. She did her best to ignore him. "Gotta get right into the studio. Got a solid offer from Enigma and one pending from Atlantic. We land that, it's a rocket to the top."

"She already said we're taking a couple months off," Cal said. "Stuff my brother's been saying about her, I don't blame her."

Dani turned her head so no one could see her tears. She missed him, still caught herself daydreaming of marrying the only man she'd given herself to. Or, at least, the only man she was sure she'd given herself to. Heroin had left some gaps. *Need some gaps. Wish Bobby was here. He'd know where to score some—stop thinking that way, Dani."*

"You think Jon airing Dani's laundry's a bad thing?" Basil snorted. "More they print, the better. Metal fans love a bad girl."

"Just shut up."

These days, even Basil obeyed her.

By the time Inferno returned stateside, Basil had won the day. The band received glowing reviews as a power trio, with all the metal magazines agreeing the subtractions only added to their sound. *Guitar Gods Magazine* featured Dani prominently in an article about up-and-coming women guitarists, telling the music world her playing would stand up with the best of them. She especially liked the lines:

While Dani Glass' visual impact is an undeniable draw, close your eyes at a live Inferno show if you can and imagine early, Zappa-era Steve Vai. Hear the difference? I wouldn't try to live off it.

"Use the traction or lose it," Basil had said.

Despite the success, Dani spent her nights pouring lonely tears into the pressure cooker until they burst into songs. The title track of Inferno's second album—"Sweet Trouble"—took less than an hour to write. She wrote the whole album in a week and a half. Now, all they had to do was record it. *With Jon and Bobby out of the picture, we might even get through it without blowing the whole advance.* She hated herself for thinking that way. *Gladly give up the advance to have him back.*

Five days and three songs into the recording process, Basil stormed into the studio, cursing a blue streak.

"Jon's suing us over the name Inferno." Once his ranting had everyone's full attention, he added, "Don't worry about it. Label has deeper pockets than Jon Ryder. They'll cut him a check and shut him up. Meantime, we have a hit record to cut."

Watching from the sound booth, Basil interrupted the third take of the fourth track, the acoustic power ballad "Still Can't Say Goodbye."

"We got bigger problems. Nobody's gonna come see Inferno if Dani starts looking like Meatloaf," he said through a mouthful of meat lover's pizza. "Diet starts today—all of you."

After two weeks of sixteen-hour days in the studio, the band was little more than half done with the album. Dani felt foggy, struggling to remember what solo to which song she was supposed to be playing at any given time. *One more week of pushing. Be a lot easier with the coke-play-heroin-sleep-rinse-repeat regimen. Wonder if my family will show up to my funeral when I end up like Bobby.*

"Solo for 'Still Can't Say Goodbye,' take eleven," the producer mumbled around his cigarette. After another botched attempt, he clapped his hand over the mic and turned to Basil. In an exaggerated whisper, he said, "Maybe it's time for one of those studio cats?"

"I've got this," Dani said, throwing her shoulders back. She set her Strat aside, took up Bobby's old Les Paul, nailed take thirteen, and collapsed onto a couch.

She woke up in a dark room.

Dani sat up, no idea where she was or how long she'd been there. Feeling sharp pain, she grasped at her forearm and yanked the needle out. *Wonder if someone shot me up and left me here, wherever here is?* She shook off a chill and screamed. "Basil? Cal? Marc? Jon? Daddy? Anyone?"

It was probably only seconds, but it felt like hours before she heard footsteps and a door opened, letting fluorescent light spill in from the hallway. Within two minutes, a pair of nurses had her calmed. Within five, they had her hooked back up to the IV.

Dani watched the clock tick off forty minutes before a balding doctor entered, a black pen resting behind his ear on a tuft of white hair. He examined her over half-moon glasses.

"You've been here just over fourteen hours," he said before she could ask.

Dani moved a shaking hand over her stomach.

"You knew?" the doctor said.

She nodded, wincing as the knots in her stomach jerked tight. "Is the…"

He shook his head, color rising on his bald crown. He seemed to struggle to keep his voice low and level. "With everything in your system… diagnosis is overdose."

"Impossible," Dani said, biting her lip until she was sure she'd drawn blood. "I haven't since I foun… since I thou… I didn't know for sure… I've been clean a month."

"Tests tell a different story." The doctor glanced over his shoulder, leaned within inches of her nose, and whispered, "Might be just as well. You have any idea what that stuff does to a baby?"

The nurses urged Dani to stay in the hospital. A counselor stopped by and suggested an outpatient detox program. They encouraged her to at least call someone to come get her. *Maybe Daddy?* They almost had her convinced until she saw herself on TV. Reporter said it was an overdose. He didn't mention the miscarriage.

For a day and a half, Dani cried and wandered the streets of Los Angeles, hiding behind dumpsters and in alleyways when cramps and spasms made walking impossible. She knew she should be hungry, but the thought of food made her want to puke.

Need some blow.

It'd be easy enough to get. *Never mind the dealers who would be all too happy to trade a balloon for a half hour with me. I could just call Basil. Don't know how, but it had to be him dosing me since Bobby died. Who else could it be?*

Cramps doubled her over.

Supposed to get better after just a few days. I can make it till then.

Dani sat in the back seat, her whole body shaking. She didn't remember calling Basil, but there he sat in the driver's seat. How long she'd been in the car or what he'd been talking about, she couldn't have said.

"Don't know why I bother," he said, tapping furiously on the steering wheel. "But hey, there's more good news—label sold out to EMI."

"We're on a major label?" Dani tried to sound enthusiastic.

He stared at her in the rearview, sneering. He seemed to think better of whatever he was going to say. "Remember that band out of Seattle?"

Dani shrugged.

"Punks got one hit and all of a sudden, the whole world's wearing flannel. EMI took up some contracts, but most of 'em were alternative and grunge bands—Nirvana wannabees. They ain't signing glam bands."

"Our record?"

"Kaput. Marc and Cal got their cut of the advance and split. Providence St. Joe's Hospital got yours. Unless I find another record company, pronto, you're back to busted."

"What good's a record company without a band?"

"You never needed 'em, kid." Basil reached back and caressed her knee. "Stick with me. I still got some ideas."

Chapter Twenty-Nine

"Never been much of a gambler," Vic said, the company's books scattered across the desk. "But we have to roll the dice if we're going to stay in business."

Greg looked over at Dad as the retired Marine stroked his stubble.

"We've been waiting for the business to come to us, and that's worked pretty good till now," Vic said. "But losing Mr. Wilkins, we either need to scale back and let people go, or we need to hit the gas."

"What're you suggesting, boss?" Greg said.

"We've always kept our eyes open for project cars, and we've always made good money on them when we've sold them. We need to expand that. Not just two or three cars—a whole lot full of them. Twenty, twenty-five to start. And we need to have rolling stock at every car show this side of the Rockies."

Dad whistled long and low. "Starting would take every dime we have."

"And then some." Vic tossed a handful of bank brochures on the desk. "I'd need you to come back in as a minority partner. No one's going to lend that kind of money to a twenty-three-year-old. We'll probably need to use the house as collateral."

"Gunny, that's not a good idea."

Tony Grassigli raised his hand slightly. Greg shushed.

"Son, this business is yours. If that's the direction we need to go, show me where to sign."

Chapter Thirty

"Where's your Caddy?" Dani said as she let herself in the passenger side of the '70s model Buick.

"Times are hard all around," Basil said. "And you need a solo demo. You can pay me back later."

"Thought they weren't signing glam acts?"

"So we buy you a lumberjack shirt. Makes no sense to me, but if that's what the kids want to see, that's what we'll give 'em. Worst case, we wait out the invasion of the flannel-wearing weirdos. How long can it possibly last?"

Dust and music flowed freely in the little studio Basil had dug up. Most of the time, Dani couldn't remember what they'd recorded the day before. Still, in less than a month, they were one song shy of Dani Glass' solo debut. Six songs, Basil said, would be perfect, allowing them to cut it for use as a demo or release it as is as an EP.

Dani couldn't remember their names, but best she could tell she got along fine with the studio musicians they'd hired. They acted like they'd known each other a long time—all but the keyboard player. He couldn't have been far out of high school and mostly kept to himself, sitting in a corner and hanging his head when not laying tracks. The others were quick enough to take Dani under their wings, talking shop and sharing whatever drugs were on the menu.

"Quit telling myself I was gonna quit years ago," said the drummer, a throwback to the early '70s with a backbeat as thick as his Southern accent.

"Yeah," Dani said, passing a laced joint. *Easier to just avoid getting pregnant again.*

A voice made Dani jump. She'd thought she was alone in the studio late at night.

"Why not just go home?" the voice repeated.

She turned, cussing a blue streak, to see a familiar face. "Stoner?"

"In the flesh. Been a fan since day one," he said, emptying a trash can. "Enough to know this ain't you. You look like hell."

"Why don't *you* go home?" It was all she could think to say.

"Got my dream job." He grabbed a push broom, starting in the corners. "Besides, I don't have a family that loves me to go back to."

The next day, Dani received an eviction notice and spent the rest of the day trying to reach Basil.

Trying to calm herself, she turned on the radio. Nothing but rap, bubble gum, or grunge. A vaguely familiar voice growled over a second-rate garage band. When the song wrapped up, the DJ announced, "That's the new one from Jon Ryder."

"Lyrics still stink," she said as she tried dialing Basil for the thousandth time.

"Look," he said when she finally reached him. "I've put everything I can into you. Hit up everyone I know. Called in every favor. No one's buying. They all say the same thing. You were just big enough in hair metal—can you believe that's what they're calling it now? You were just big enough we can't sell you as a grunge act. Word 'poseur' came up a lot. Face it, kid, you're busted. Time to go home."

"Can't." Dani needed a hit of something. Blow, preferably, but any port in a storm. "Got anything to settle my nerves?"

"I'll give you a lift."

"No way I could face my father like this."

"You're outta options, kid. But who knows? Maybe this Seattle thing will pass, and we can try again in six months."

Dani gulped hard, holding her hands tight to her jeans to keep them from shaking. "What about *Playboy*?"

Chapter Thirty-One

"Not long ago, I worried about keeping the doors open," Vic said. "Now, my worries are finding employees to handle the workload. Any car salesmen looking for work in the house?"

A chuckle rippled through the crowd. There were no fewer than five car dealers at the breakfast.

"The just man walketh in his integrity," Vic read to the suits and ties gathered at Broken Yolk Breakfast Nook. "His children are blessed after him."

Setting his shiny new black leather Bible on the table, Vic thanked the Full Gospel Business Men's Fellowship for the opportunity to bring the morning's devotional. "The turnaround of Fidelis Classic motors can all be credited to the blessings of God passed on to me by my father, who walks in integrity. He served his country as a Marine. He served his customers and built the company by word of mouth. And it was the fact that his integrity was known far and wide that allowed us to take the steps we needed to take to recover after a difficult stretch. I am blessed, and I know someday my children will be blessed because my dad walked in his integrity."

By the time the meal was done, Vic had three invitations to speak at other chapters of the Christian business organization, two invitations to preach, and one burning desire—to build his business to the point that he could turn it over to someone else and turn his attention back to preaching the gospel.

Vic whistled an old hymn as he left the prayer breakfast. *I can juggle business and ministry a few more years if I need to. There'll be plenty of chances to go on missions trips and do other short-term missions work.* Contrary to everything he'd expected, sacrificing ministry goals to build his father's business actually gained him opportunities to preach.

"Lord, your plans are always better than mine," he prayed as a Prevost Coach pulled into the parking lot, a giant image of Jon Ryder screaming into a microphone stretching from top to bottom on both sides. He'd had his hair cut and wore brown flannel, but there was no mistaking Dani's boyfriend.

"Day keeps getting better," he said, adding a silent prayer of thanks. *Maybe Dani's on board.* He'd been praying for another chance to talk with her since the limo drove by the house that night. Might not have been her, Pastor Stenger said when they'd talked about it, but who else would drive a stretched Cadillac down his street in Rio Flaco?

The side door opened just as Vic reached the bus, and Jon stepped out, shielding his eyes against the light.

"You get one phone call."

Vic had never felt so sore.

The arresting officer hadn't cared what names the victim had used for his sister. He hadn't cared what kinds of details the victim had spouted of the things his sister had done. He hadn't cared that the victim had drawn a crowd or even that the victim had placed himself within two inches of Vic's nose.

The arresting officer cared that Vic hadn't stopped the ground and pound when told to do so. He hadn't cared whether Vic heard him.

"Don't ask any questions," Vic said when Greg answered the shop phone. "Come bail me out of the County Jail. Whatever you do, don't say anything to Dad."

The first cancellation was waiting on the answering machine when Vic got to the office. The pastor had seen the whole fight. By the end of the day, he'd received four more cancellations. The pastors and organization leaders were no more impressed with his reasons than the officer had been.

"Hello," Vic mumbled into the phone, expecting another cancellation. Just business, this time. More cars coming in. Big account, almost as big as the Wilkins account.

Big deal.

By that night, his fight and arrest were all over the local news. The next day, the Associated Press picked up the headline:

Part-time preacher publicly pounds rock star.

The story, published all over the country, painted him as a religious nut who had stalked the singer waiting for revenge for dating his sister, whom the paper described as pursuing a solo career after the breakup of Inferno—the first Vic had heard of the band's demise.

"At least there's some good news in all this."

Chapter Thirty-Two

"Dunno what to tell you," Basil said. "You'd have to do a lot more than sing for me to keep you in nose candy. This point, you're costing me money."

Dani had been shaking for two days. "What about *Play*—"

"Been trying hard not to tell you. Three months ago, they'd have written you a check with six figures. Now, you're not even a has-been. You're an almost-was."

"I need a fix."

"Fix? You need to pay rent." Basil started to say something, hesitated, and started back toward the door. "Tell you what, there's some other rags that might give you a few bucks. Not very classy, though. Didn't think you'd be willing—"

"Set it up. I don't care."

Three days later, Dani sipped whiskey and counted her money in a seedy LA bar, vaguely aware of a band running sound checks in the corner. She couldn't believe what she'd done for a couple shots of heroin and just enough cash to stop the eviction proceedings. She scratched the red welts rising on her arm. She'd never injected before and part of her worried about sharing that needle with the other girls. But it had been the only way she could afford it. *And who cares? Maybe better if it ends anyway.*

"Take a number, I'm full," Dani said over her shoulder as someone sat on the next barstool over. She hadn't paid for any of her drinks yet and didn't expect to. She was still pretty enough for that, at least.

Whoever it was didn't relocate, so she turned to face him. Fresh-faced kid. Definitely didn't belong here. Something familiar about him.

"Played keys on your record," he said. "You look terrible."

"Thanks."

"This is my last gig in this kind of place," the kid said, ordering a Coke. "Gave my life to Christ just before we did your record and I've never felt quite right about it since."

"Don't want to hear it." Dani drained the shot glass.

"Neither did I, but you need to," The kid said, sipping his soda and trying to make eye contact. "Look, that clown that represents you told me you were a choir girl when he found you. Thought it was real funny. Kept lacing your drinks. Thought that was funny, too." The kid hung his head. "Guess I should have said something then."

Dani tapped her glass on the bar and pointed at the kid when the bartender approached.

"He can play in the band, but he can't buy you no drinks."

Neither could she, technically, but no one had carded her. Dani fished out a five, glaring at the kid as the bartender poured. "You're getting expensive to have around."

"Look, I'm just saying. The guy said he had to get a restraining order to keep your brother away. Maybe you should just go—"

"Maybe you should go to hell!"

"Already been." The kid pushed away from the bar. "Never going back. You don't have to, either."

Dani considered calling a cab. *You'd think, of all places, I could avoid being preached at in a bar. Really should go home, anyway.* She'd drank more than usual and knew she was going to regret it in the morning. *I can figure out what comes next later. Maybe more photo shoots.* She shuddered. She'd never felt so degraded, even around Basil. *Oh well, at least they're small publications.* One of them wasn't even a real publication. It was for some new thing called the Web or something like that. Only a handful of computer nerds even knew anything about it. *No one I know will ever see them. And if I downgrade, I might be able to find a dumpy apartment I can afford that way.*

Across the bar, a worn-out woman laughed at the attention men on either side of her offered. She looked like she'd been pretty once, now a hollow-cheeked bleach blonde with way too much eyeshadow and tracks running the length of her skinny arms.

I need a fix.

The lady wouldn't share, but she told Dani where to find her dealer. San Julian Street. Dani had never been to Skid Row. She'd never needed to buy her own drugs. She jingled her keys and stumbled out the door.

ani walked back to her car with six balloons of heroin and a plan to pay the rent. She'd had the solution all along and couldn't believe she hadn't thought of it. *Bobby's Les Paul.* Even at a pawn shop, it would bring in enough for a couple months' rent—longer if she downgraded from the band's flat. *Too much apartment for just me, anyway. Might even be able to trade for a secondhand Peavey or some other decent-but-not-classic guitar and still walk away with enough to keep a roof over my head.*

She found herself wondering where Bobby got the guitar in the first place. He'd never said. *Never even seemed to realize what he had.* She felt a twinge of guilt about pawning it. After all, Bobby's mom said he'd wanted her to have it. *But Bobby's gone, and you can't eat sentiments, much less shoot them up. Besides, maybe I can get it back after a few more photo shoots.*

Her stomach churned. *Maybe I could get a real job instead. Not like I don't have any skills. Gotta be a body shop that would hire me somewhere in LA.*

Dani got in the car and pulled a balloon from her pocket. *Better wait till I get home. If this stuff's as good as the guy said, I won't be able to drive after. Still pretty buzzed as it is.*

Half a mile from home, red-and-blue lights flooded Dani's rearview mirror.

❝Yeah, driving under the influence ain't the half of it," LAPD Officer Brown said to the booking officer as he guided Dani toward the counter by the cuffs behind her back. "Six balloons. And stolen property. Get this—remember that guitar stolen out of Lieutenant Yates' car three years ago? Let's just say I'm on the fast track to make sergeant."

"Yeah, well tell it to the new kid," the booking officer said. "Time for my smoke break."

Dani stared at her shoes. She could hear the ear-to-ear grin in the officer's voice as he recounted the story of his big catch for the benefit of the booking officer's replacement. He was in the middle of explaining all about the lieutenant's missing guitar and how the perp claimed a friend had given it to her. "Amazing, ain't it, just how many people give stolen stuff away?"

"Dani?" A familiar female voice.

Her head throbbed, and every muscle turned to jelly as her eyes adjusted to the fluorescent lighting.

"Julie?"

"You two know each other? This story just keeps getting better."

Julie's voice was strained as she walked Dani through the fingerprinting, mug shot, and paperwork.

"You're in serious trouble, you know?" she whispered. "If that guitar's worth more than one thousand dollars, you're looking at a felony. And six balloons? They could charge you with intent to distribute."

Dani kept her eyes on her socks. They'd taken her shoes.

"You get a phone call. Number still the same?"

Dani heard her start to dial.

"Don't call home! Here, call 226-9630."

Julie shook her head. "What happened?"

"Just give me my call. Please."

Chapter Thirty-Three

Vic finally broke down and spent the extra money to have caller ID installed at home and in the office. Why Jon Ryder got such a kick out of calling and harassing him with the gory details about Dani was beyond him, but it was easier to keep it from Dad by shutting off the answering machine and screening calls. So far, he'd ignored seventy calls. His lawyer had suggested keeping a tally, saying it could be a mitigating factor when he faced his court date.

He didn't recognize the number on the display now—an LA number. *Could be Dani.* He flipped the answering machine back on, the hair on the back of his arms standing to attention at the voice on the other end.

"Vic, I shouldn't be doing this, but we need to talk. Call me. 213-228-1991."

"You're right. You shouldn't, Julie."

"Here, take Caleb," Kari said, handing Vic one squalling baby through the door while another fussed inside Shelly's apartment. "And c'mon in."

"What do I do with it?" Vic hollered over the baby's escalating screams as Kari cooed the other's name—Joshua—in a vain attempt to settle him down.

"Feed him, burp him, change him, rock him, sing to him, who knows?" Kari said. "Do something. Shelly's in class until ten."

Great. Two hours. Vic tried rocking the baby. Only seemed to set him off. Cooing his name didn't fare much better, and all attempts to give him a bottle were summarily rejected. *Doesn't look like Kari and I are going to get much talking in.*

After an hour of stereophonic squalling, Vic started rethinking the brood he'd imagined. Half an hour more and the babies had cried themselves out. Vic glanced down at Caleb, sprawled on his shoulder, drooling. "Everyone ought to have a couple of these."

Kari flashed one of those eye-smiles over her glasses, kissing him softly as she tucked the babies in.

Vic had a ton he wanted to unload. He reminded himself to tell her that Julie had been calling. Not that he felt he'd done anything wrong, or even that it would have been wrong to talk with her, but he didn't want any secrets between them. *After all, in a couple months, I'm going to ask her.*

He was just working his way up to telling her when Shelly arrived, waking the babies and starting a whole new round. By the time they'd helped Shelly feed and burp and coo, Kari had fallen asleep on the couch. Smiling and covering her with an afghan, Vic agreed with Shelly that it was best to leave her there. *I'll just talk with her after church.*

As morning rolled into afternoon, Vic sat on the front porch with a glass of lemonade, Teddy Bear lounging at his feet. It was the first Saturday he'd taken off in months. A couple of the shop's recent hires were outside San Fran promoting the business at a classic car show, the bills were paid—finally caught up—and he had nothing so pressing that it couldn't wait for Monday. Dad was at the shop, finishing up the detailing on a new client's Model A—the most beautiful specimen Vic had ever seen. Vic had offered to help, but Dad insisted he didn't need to be babysat. *Good to see him cranky again.*

Julie had tried calling him twice already, but he'd let the answering machine get it. He had to talk himself down when he heard her voice. "Not a good idea. Glad she's saved now, but it wouldn't be right to ask her to be a preacher's wife. Besides, a bird in the hand…"

Teddy Bear slapped his tail against the porch, stretching and giving himself a shake. He nudged Vic as a car pulled in the driveway.

Julie.

There was no pretending he wasn't there. His palms started to sweat as she took a spot next to him on the bench and waited a whole minute before deadpanning, "You're ignoring me."

"You can't skip town and expect me to wait here with bells on."

Inside, the phone rang.

"Oh, *now* you're answering it?" Julie said, following him.

"Depends." He checked the Caller ID. "It's the office."

"It'll wait." Julie stood in the doorway, hands on hips.

Vic did his level best not to think about how good she looked in a T-shirt and jeans.

"It's about Dani," she said. "Let's go back outside."

As he followed her, Kari's Yugo pulled in. The briefest look told him all he needed to know about how she'd take it. Kari's mascara was already running when she slammed into reverse and squealed out of the driveway.

"You're going to want to sit down," Julie said as Vic took a couple steps toward the retreating Yugo. The phone started ringing again. "It'll wait."

Vic fished his keys out of his pocket.

"Dani's in trouble."

"Thought you had news." He headed toward his car as Kari sped off. *First time I've seen her break the speed limit. Or any rule.*

"Serious trouble."

Vic's head was on a swivel, looking back and forth between Julie and the Yugo's fading taillights. Squatting on the porch step, he flashed an out-with-it stare.

"Legally, I shouldn't be here. Dani told me not to tell you."

"Look, I can't help Dani. Her manager put a restraining order on us."

"Just thought you'd like to know—" Julie said as a shiny Dodge Ram screeched to a stop at the curb.

Greg leaned out the window, spewing a string of profanities about not answering the phone. "Get to the hospital! Now! Gunny's hurt!"

"You really should know," Julie said, cut off with a wave of Vic's hand.

"It'll wait," he said, hopping in the pickup.

"She's been arrested!" she hollered after him as the truck spit gravel.

"Getting to be a family pastime," Greg said as he sped off.

Chapter Thirty-Four

"Face it, until this grunge thing passes, this is your reality," Basil said, matter-of-factly. "Only two ways you could possibly repay me, and you've already said no to one of 'em a thousand times. Unless you've changed your—"

"No." Dani hung her head, refusing to even look at the strip club entrance. "Rather go back to jail."

"Suit yourself. You called me."

Dani looked out her window so Basil wouldn't see her tears.

"Not like you're daddy's little girl anymore. If you was, you'd have called him," Basil said. "Welcome to the real world, where you owe me real money. This place ain't so bad. Owner's an old friend of mine. Ask for Ace. Tell him who you are, and he'll set you up. Couple months, you'll have me paid back. Maybe by then, kids will start listening to real music again."

Chapter Thirty-Five

Dani felt numb. The faces of thousands of men blurred together. The teenagers who greased bouncers' palms and snuck in with fake IDs. Middle-aged men who didn't bother taking their wedding rings off. Men older than her grandfather. All leering. All laughing. All staring. All grabbing. All offering a pittance to see a fallen star at her lowest.

She pretended she was dancing in front of arena crowds again. But no one was here to hear her sing or play guitar. Her hands shook so badly she doubted she could perform even if she had one to play. It would be easy enough to get a fix, but she needed to be clean.

The trembling, the shakes, the bad dreams. None of those compared with the worst withdrawal symptoms—her mind beginning to clear. *Wish I could just fade into oblivion.*

"You know, you still have a name people know," that ape of a man, Ace Davis, said one night in the dressing area. "There's people out there who would pay anything to be up close and personal with a celebrity— even a has-been B-lister. Gives 'em a story to tell. Say the word. I'll pay Basil off and get you making some real money."

She needed it. Her court date loomed just around the corner. *No way the public defender's going to keep me out of jail. No way I can afford anyone else as long as Ace gives my pay directly to Basil.* She hid as much of her tip money as she dared and it was starting to add up, but even that would disappear if Basil ever found out about it. And as long as he paid her rent, he called the shots.

"Can't," Dani said, looking at her toes.

"Suit yourself," Ace said, petting her bare shoulder. "But you could make as much in half an hour as you make all night dancing."

Dani felt dry heaves coming on.

"Change your mind, let me know. Offer has an expiration date. You wasn't that big a celebrity and you ain't getting no better looking."

After a month of dancing, Dani had managed to squirrel away just enough for a second-rate lawyer. *Maybe I can get off with probation.* Stopping for a Slurpee on her way to take him the retainer fee, she noticed a neon green poster in the 7-Eleven window:

Bucket O' Bolts Classic Car Show. Saturday and Sunday, April 25-26.

She caught herself smiling, hugging herself. Daddy had taken her to that show every year since they'd been in California unless he was deployed. It was almost a month away.

"Maybe I'll go."

"Hey, girl, don't I know you?"

Three teens in sideways baseball caps with matching blue bandanas tied around their left legs towered over her shoulder.

"Yeah, you know her, Cuz," the shortest of them said. "Seen her in the club."

"Oh yeah, she the one that won't dance up close." He smiled, showing off a pair of gold teeth.

Dani tried to return the smile as she clutched her purse and tried to slip past.

"She close now."

Filing a police report didn't change much.

She wondered if the officer who grilled her was old enough to shave. *At least it's not Julie.* The best description Dani could give matched a hundred profiles the LAPD were already looking for, the officer admitted. But they'd see what they could do. He didn't give her much hope they'd be able to recover her money.

"Any idea how many hookers get robbed over there?"

"I'm not a prostitute."

The officer looked her outfit up and down and appeared to think better of arguing the matter. "You're lucky to be alive. What were you doing carrying two thousand cash in that neighborhood anyway?"

"You can't go on like that," Ace said when she showed up to work that night. "Looks like you went fifteen rounds with Mike Tyson."

"They don't look so good, either," Dani mumbled through swollen lips.

"Bet they don't, but that don't help me."

"I need the money. Basil said he's done helping."

"Breaks my heart, but business is business."

"I'll be on the streets."

Ace shrugged.

Dani turned to walk away, afraid of the dark for the first time in her life.

"Hold on, kid. Got a place you can stay till you heal up. Meanwhile, got a couple clients won't care so much if your face looks like hamburger long as they can see they was with Dani Glass. Offer's still on the table, but it won't be tomorrow."

Chapter Thirty-Six

"How's Gunny?"

Points for consistency. Greg started his Monday the same as he'd started every Monday the last couple months. "He's got lots of time to think," Vic said.

"That's never good."

"He's going stir crazy," Vic said. "And it'll be at least another month before the doctor will clear him to come back to work. But hey, in the meantime, we've got work to do. Need you to cover the Bucket O' Bolts Show for me next weekend."

"In LA? No can do. It's my weekend with little Greg."

"Dad was going to go. We need to be represented."

"Have a good time."

"Not likely," Vic snorted. "I'll be in court."

Greg softened his tone. "Wish I could help. Let's just send a couple of the guys. Zach's coming along. Have him take a helper and go."

"Need someone who can sign a check. Got a line on some rolling stock I want you to bring back."

"I'm not canceling on my son again."

"Take him with you."

"He's three."

"So was Dani at her first car show."

"Heard from her lately?"

Vic pulled out a legal pad, jotting down names, contacts, and details about what he wanted purchased. "You know a deal when you see one. If we can make money, pull the trigger. Company checkbook's yours."

That night, Teddy Bear ran idiot laps around Vic's car when he pulled into the driveway.

"What are you doing outside?"

The dog heaved himself against the door, whining. Dad's car was in the garage, but no lights were on inside the house.

Vic rushed inside, calling for Dad. No answer. The day's mail sat on the kitchen counter, where Dad always set it before going through it. A large yellow envelope lay open on top, addressed to "Sargint Tony Grassigli." No return address.

"Dad?" Vic called again, heading into the living room.

Dad lay twisted on a pile of glass shards in front of the remains of the family TV set, his wheelchair overturned. Dried blood covered his arms and hands, still clenched into fists, and his breath came in ragged gasps.

Vic spent the night and most of the next day at the hospital. The doctor told him this morning that Dad might not have made it if he'd lost any more blood. Vic still didn't have any clear idea what had happened. They were able to repair the lacerated artery in Dad's arm, but the doctor felt it best to keep him sedated a while longer.

Visitors had been in and out. Pastor Stenger's visit was awkward, and Vic was glad it didn't last long. He was glad for Greg's company and would have liked him to stay longer, but someone had to run the shop. Others came and went, some carrying flowers or cards, others offering what encouragement they could. A few suggested Vic needed to take better care of his father. One took the occasion to scold him for skipping out on church the last couple months.

And then, Shelly showed up, right around dinner time.

"I'm not much of a cook," she said, offering a bowl covered with aluminum foil, "but I figured you'd be ready for anything but hospital food."

Vic took the bowl without a word, setting it on the chair beside him. Shelly rocked on her heels, started to say something, then appeared to think better of it. She repeated the ritual half a dozen times.

"If you have something to say—"

"Kari misses you."

"She need a spokesperson these days?"

"Why are you avoiding her?"

"My dad's in a hospital bed—"

"And she should be here with you. Clearly, that other girl—"

"Julie's history."

"That was fast."

"Excuse me, Mr. Grassigli?" an orderly said before Vic could retort. "You have a phone call. Take it at the desk."

"You see it?" a muffled voice demanded, laughing when he picked up the phone.

"See what? Who is this?" Vic waved Shelly off as she approached.

"Don't play dumb." The line went dead.

Vic turned back to Shelly, her arms crossed. "Don't you have kids to take care of?"

She turned on her heel. "You never deserved Kari anyway."

"Wait," Vic said. She didn't. He followed. "There was nothing going on with Julie. She stopped by to tell me something about Dani. Dad got hurt and I—"

Vic ran into Shelly as she spun around. "What happened to Dani?"

"Don't know. Never called Julie back."

Shelly took a step back. "You really need to give Kari a call."

"Don't have time for someone who doesn't trust me."

"Give her a break. You don't know what she's been through. No one here does."

That night, Vic stopped by Blockbuster and picked up *Not Without My Daughter* on the way home. Before the blowup, Kari had wanted to watch it together. He figured he'd fall asleep watching it.

Remembering the TV was busted, Vic hauled in the small set from the garage and set it up with the VHS player in his room. It took him three attempts at putting the tape in to realize there was already something in the machine. *Odd.* Dad was an absolute stickler about removing and rewinding videos. Vic had twice lost TV privileges for a month for that very offense.

Vic ejected the tape, a home-recorded tape labeled "Dani" with little hearts in hot pink marker. *Doesn't look like Dani's handwriting.*

Vic popped it back in.

A second and a half in, he ripped the VCR out of the wall and threw it across the room. No one should see his sister like that.

Or his daughter.

Chapter Thirty-Seven

Dani believed her life couldn't sink any lower than working at the strip club. She was wrong.

Night after night, she saw a revolving cast of revolting men willing to hand Ace wads of sweaty cash for an hour of her time and a story they could tell the world.

Some talked sweet. Some hit her. Given her choice, she preferred the mean ones.

Pigs, all of them.

She never saw any of the money Ace promised, though he did keep her just deep enough in heroin to stave off the worst of the cravings.

At first, she'd threatened to run.

"Door's open," he said. "You'll be back."

She'd even tried putting out job applications at first. Garages and car dealerships wrote her off. She finally found two body shops willing to hire a woman. One checked her criminal record. The other wanted her to take a drug test.

Even McDonald's turned her down.

Ace just laughed at her when he found out.

"You don't even want to know what the stuff you're shooting is laced with," he said as he handed her a needle and spoon. "You've never heard of withdrawals like you'll have if you stop. You ain't going nowhere."

Her life became a nonstop attempt to stay numb.

Dani's court date passed three weeks before she checked a calendar and remembered she was supposed to go. *Who cares? At this point, jail might be a relief.*

Have I been living in Ace's apartment for months? Years? It would have been easier for Dani to tell how many times she'd shot up. She could still count those, the pinpricks lining her arms, legs, and neck.

The woman staring at her from inside the mirror looked like she was in her forties. Hollow eyes. Sunken cheeks. Clumps of hair missing.

"Do something with yourself," Ace hollered down the stairs. "Special visitors coming in a couple hours."

She knew better than to argue. She'd tried calling his bluff once, and he'd cut her off. She shuddered, remembering what had seemed like days of violent shaking and vomiting. Even that wasn't as bad as the indescribable things she'd seen when she went more than a few hours without a hit.

She did what she could with makeup and hairspray.

The woman in the mirror frightened her, threatened her, then softened her tone.

"You know," she rasped, "you could just end it all."

"Can I have something to eat first?" Ace had to be able to hear her stomach growling.

"I'll order pizza when you're done. Can't keep customers waiting."

Dani heard someone upstairs. "You should play her the new song."

Basil?

Chuckling.

That's Jon's laugh.

"Why not? It's all about her."

"No," Dani whispered.

Ace faced her.

"No," Dani said, looking at the ground.

"Whatever." Ace headed upstairs. "You boys take your time."

Dani lost her breath as Jon filled the doorway above. He wore ripped bell bottoms and a flannel shirt, and his hair was mussed, but there was no mistaking that smile.

"Wow," Basil said, following Jon downstairs and standing over Dani. "I'd have given an arm for this a year ago. Now, I want my money back."

Jon laughed.

"I loved you." Dani stood, meeting the singer's eyes.

"So did lots of chicks." Looking at Basil, he said, "I'll pass, too. Got to get to the studio anyway."

Dani took a step after him. "I loved you."

"It was fun," he said over his shoulder.

"I loved you."

"I loved me, too."

Chapter Thirty-Eight

D ad never talked about what he'd seen on the tape and Vic wasn't about to bring it up, even though he'd heard rumors of copies distributed all over the country through underground channels.

And there was no escaping the sordid details laid out in "Dani's Song." As far as Vic knew, Jon Ryder's song hadn't hit it big on a national level, but it was inescapable locally. Vic had only heard it once, but that was plenty. He spent days trying to get the hook out of his head:

> *"When the church bells ring,*
> *Oh man, could Dani sing,*
> *But when the lights turned low and it was time to go*
> *She would come alive*
> *And make me lose control*
> *When she would..."*

How they got away with playing the lyrics that followed on the radio was beyond him.

Vic believed the people at church were trying to be understanding. Most of them, anyway. They had known Dani when she was that impulsive but mostly innocent girl leading the singing. They tried not to show resentment for the negative light in which the popular song painted their church.

A few were less charitable. Vic heard the whispers and imagined the things he didn't hear were even harsher. He hadn't received an invitation to preach in months, undoubtedly because of the trouble Dani had brought on their family.

Between those things and the discomfort of facing Kari, Vic adopted the habit of being busy on Sundays. Dad still went to church most weeks. *Wonder who sits with him. If anyone.*

"Not like I don't have lots of things to do," Vic reminded himself constantly. Fidelis Restoration and Auto Sales was booming, and he was looking at expanding operations to include a real-deal car dealership—new cars and used. He'd already received positive responses from the Big Three. At this point, all he had to do was decide between Ford, Chrysler, and GM and sign his autograph at the bank. They'd have to put the entire restoration business up as collateral, but he had no doubt Dad would sign. In a matter of months, he could open Rio Flaco's first new car dealership.

"Grassigli Auto. I like the sound of that."

He only hoped Dani hadn't damaged the name so much that it would hurt business. Then again, Dani used a stage name, and Vic doubted most people outside of their church circles would associate the Grassigli name with the mud she'd dragged it through. It hadn't stopped anyone from doing business with him so far—other than churches—though he did occasionally have to field uncomfortable questions.

His standard answer had become, "I don't know where Dani is. Or if she is anymore. She never looked back. I hope she's okay."

He couldn't allow himself much time to think about Dani beyond that. He had a business to run. And this afternoon, he had a court date to keep.

The sun peeked over the clouded horizon, painting a dazzling display of purple and crimson that Dani barely noticed as she picked through the dumpster for yesterday's McNuggets. Ace threw her out two nights ago. Or was it three? Something about her being of no use.

Most of the time, she wasn't sure if she was awake or having another nightmare. When cravings came, and they came often, she wondered whether she could turn tricks somewhere. A couple times, she'd tried, but no one seemed interested, and other girls ran her off.

She considered trying to find some legitimate work. But no one was going to take her seriously until she'd cleaned up and had a shower. And working while going through withdrawals? *What in the world could I do with my hands shaking like this?*

Right now, she was sure the cramps in her stomach were from want of food rather than drugs, though she wouldn't have turned down a fix if she could get her hands on one. She scarfed anything edible she could find, afraid one of the workers would see her and run her off like they had yesterday.

When they did, she wandered the streets. She knew she was dirty. Knew she was drawing stares as the city came to life. She kept her head down and walked wherever her feet took her.

By midmorning, she found herself roaming through a sea of classic cars. *Or am I just having a good dream for a change, remembering better days?*

She plopped under an oak tree with a good view of an orange GTO and a white-and-blue '69 ½ Trans Am convertible. *Just like Daddy's.* How in the world anyone had found it was beyond her. *Only seven others that look like it in the whole world other than Daddy's. Only three others like it if you pop the hood.*

Out of the corner of her eye, she saw an overdressed crowd gathering. Lots of suits and dresses. A few tuxedos. *Why would anyone dress up for a car show?* She sighed. *Knew it was just me dreaming.*

Still, dream or no dream, she was content to sit and look at the old Pontiac, imagining herself in it, remembering countless hours staying up late with Daddy, scraping, sanding, puttying, sanding, painting his other baby until it was perfect. *Dream's going to take a horrific turn soon enough. They always do.*

"God, if only this could be real."

Wedding music played behind her. She closed her eyes when a glowing woman in white marched through the well-dressed crowd. She gulped, forcing memories of a dream out of her heart as the words of the preacher reached her. The rest of the crowd didn't seem to notice her, but she was sure the minister was looking straight at her, tormenting her, taunting her with something about the holiness and blessedness of the marriage bed.

She closed her eyes when the bride was lifted into the GTO's passenger seat, but she couldn't drown out the engine's distinctive sound as it drove off. She stuffed her mouth with french fries she'd stashed in her pocket to keep from screaming.

Vic thanked his lawyer. The judge had considered his sister's relationship with the victim, and the terms of his probation wouldn't stop him from continuing to work and build his business.

Dani woke and wiped drool from her chin. She had no idea how long she'd dozed under the tree. When her eyes cleared, the first thing they settled on was Julie, in jeans and T-shirt, walking, eating cotton candy, and laughing with some guy who looked a lot like Vic. Her head throbbed, and she blinked several times, squinting against the fading sunlight. At first, she wasn't sure. Maybe it was her brother. *Nah, not unless he grew six inches,* she thought as they got closer.

Less than half the classic cars remained and, every now and then, people loaded cars onto trailers. If it was anything like the shows she'd been to in years past, the cars would trickle off until just a few were left, the owners still buying, selling, and swapping stories until morning.

Still fifty yards off, Julie didn't seem to have noticed her yet. *Julie can't see me. I missed my court date.*

She let that sink in. Maybe jail wouldn't be so bad. The food had to be better than dumpster salvage. Images of a cage, of Ace's basement, flashed rapid-fire through her brain. She turned her back to the couple and walked, hoping her brisk pace would put enough distance between them that she could run for it if Julie spotted her.

She was about to venture a peek over her shoulder when a pair of uniformed cops stopped and talked to people in the crowd ahead. *Looking for something. Or someone.*

Dani drew a sharp breath, eyes darting to either side of the road, looking for a side street, an alley, anywhere she could hide. She almost bumped into a man carrying a toddler on his shoulders.

Greg?!

He made brief eye contact and smiled, but Dani didn't see recognition in his eyes. He continued past, laughing and pointing out features of the remaining cars to the boy, who clapped his hands and asked three questions for every one Greg answered.

The cops! They were getting closer. If they hadn't seen her yet, they would soon. Over her shoulder, she saw she hadn't made much headway. Julie looked another direction but continued walking straight toward her. *Bet that guy with her is a plainclothes cop. She's here to find me. They're all here to find me. She thinks I don't know her little plan.*

A cramp socked Dani in the gut, doubling her over. *Got to be somewhere I can get a balloon of heroin. No time to think about that now. Got to hide.*

A pair of red pickups with three-car hauler trailers bore the familiar Fidelis logo. One was full, the other carried two cars – a '53 Ford and that orange GTO from the wedding. *Looks just like mine did.*

Dani scrambled to the other side of the trailer, alternately squatting and peering through the car windows to see that she hadn't been followed. As quietly as she could, she climbed onto the trailer and tried the GTO's door. Unlocked. Crawling in, she lay on the back-seat floor and tried to slow her breathing. She could see the tops of people's heads, but none of them wore the shielded LAPD cap.

As she lay there breathing a sigh of relief, something under the driver's seat caught her eye. *Looks like an old 8-track cassette.* She fished it out: The DeGarmo & Key Band's *Straight On*, with a photo of her favorite guitar player, Dana Key, front and center sporting feathered hair and a big mustache.

My 8-track. My car. Smells like new.

She turned the 8-track over and read the track listing.

PROGRAM I
JERICHO
LET HIM HELP YOU TODAY

PROGRAM II
BAD LIVIN'
I NEVER KNEW YOU

Scanning down to PROGRAM IV, she read aloud, "'Livin' on the Edge of Dyin'… I sure have been."

She shushed herself when some kid outside said, "That car has a pretty voice."

She knew the laugh that answered. Greg.

"Cars don't talk."

She tried to keep her eyes open. Felt herself fading. Shuddered. Knew a nightmare crept over her shoulder.

Help me today.

Chapter Thirty-Nine

Vic gritted his teeth, refusing to speak the words invading his mind as the wrench clanged to the floor and red splotches formed on his greasy knuckles. Underneath the car, the new guy moved his head slightly to avoid the wrench and kept working.

What's his name again?

Vic hated asking employees to work Sunday. Dad never would have allowed it. But he had worked the last three months of Sundays, and they were still behind. Between him and two of his newest employees, they needed to get the '39 Continental to start by tomorrow.

"It's a blessing to be busy," Vic reminded himself as he wiped his knuckles clean. "Means there's provision."

"Appreciate the OT," What's-his-name grunted, shoving the oil pan back into place.

"We get the dealership open, there'll be plenty of it—and raises for everyone."

Vic knew the numbers backward and forward. He knew they were already paying most of their people twenty percent over going rates. *But that's how you keep good people.* "When a company prospers, its workers ought to prosper with it."

"Wish everyone thought that way."

Vic hadn't realized he was thinking out loud. "If my Dad had raised them, they would." Looking at his watch, he called across the room, "Hey Brian, didn't your daughter have a dance recital or something? Wash up and get out of here. We'll handle this."

ani shielded her eyes against the first rays of crimson sunrise flooding through the GTO windows. Between cramps, lying faceup on the hard floorboard, dry heaves, a thousand thoughts and fears assaulting her, and a pair of mosquitoes she didn't dare move to swat, Dani hadn't slept a wink. For more than an hour last night, she'd listened to Greg talking and laughing with what she could only guess were new Fidelis employees. Whoever they were, they sounded happy to be part of the team.

Although everything had been quiet since sundown, she didn't dare make a sound. *Jon. Basil. Ace. Julie. The LAPD. They're all out there, I just know it. Just waiting for their chance to drag me out of the car and take me God-knows-where. But I'll fool them. I'll go the one place they'll never think to look for me... home. I'm still a heck of a mechanic. And if I can ever get my hands to stop shaking, I know I can be as good as I ever was. My father's workers all drive nice cars. They all have food to eat. My father always takes care of them. I can never be Daddy's little girl again, but so what? Maybe if I admit I was wrong, he'll feel sorry for me and give me a job. If I can get a job, I can lay low until they stop looking for me. Maybe he'll even let me sleep in the shop until I can get a place.*

The truck engine rumbled to life and Dani braced herself. When the truck and trailer hit the highway, Dani mustered the courage to climb onto the bench seat and lie down. She stretched, working cramps out of her limbs. *Keep your head down, dummy. No one can see you. This is dumb. Daddy can't see me like this. Ever. Be easier to throw myself off a bridge. But this is the only chance I've got.*

She curled into a ball and cried herself to sleep. *Can always kill myself after if he won't put me to work.*

Chapter Forty

Dani's stomach alternated between grumbling and cramping, providing her only reminder of the passing time. She knew she needed food, but she wanted heroin. She tried to remember how long it had been, how long she'd heard the physical withdrawals lasted.

From time to time, she allowed herself a peek out the window. Daddy's Trans Am rode behind her GTO on the trailer. Peering over the headrest through the windshield, she could see Greg's head bobbing left and right in the cab. *Wonder what he's listening to? Could go for some music about now.*

She still had her key after all this time. She considered climbing up front and turning the car radio on. She laughed at the thought of flipping between channels to try to figure out which station Greg was bopping in sync to. *Known him almost four years and I don't even know what kind of music he likes.*

An off-the-charts cramp derailed her train of thought. For what seemed like hours, Dani could do nothing but lay still, doubled over and groaning.

The grumbling overtook the cramps as she watched a Denny's sign come into view. She forced herself to stop groaning as the truck hissed to a stop, its doors slamming. A child sang a song she didn't recognize. Something about women being the death of him.

"Probably shouldn't sing that one." Greg laughed as he said it. "Not sure your momma will appreciate it when I drop you off."

"Day-ad," the child said, making two syllables of it. "Why was the orange car talking this morning?"

Dani put her hands over her mouth as dry heaves overtook her. Greg and the kid were going to pass right by her on their way into the restaurant.

"Suppose it didn't like waking up early any better than you did," Greg said, bringing on fits of laughter. The boy's curly locks appeared in the window as Greg hoisted him onto his shoulders and he pointed at her as they walked by. She held her breath as the boy tapped Greg's shoulder, daring to breathe only after they had passed by.

Dani had no idea where they were, though she was pretty sure they were still headed to Rio Flaco. *Can't risk having that kid convince Greg to look in the car.* She considered shutting herself in the trunk but remembered the day when she was little and Daddy had come home early and hugged her tighter than usual. She found out later from Vic that one of the Marines Daddy served with had a son who locked himself in the trunk and died. The boy had just wanted to go camping with his dad and his buddies. They looked for him for three days, never thinking to check the trunk until the smell alerted them.

Maybe I should just change cars. But her father's Trans Am was the only one she had a key for. She couldn't bring herself to sit in it.

By the time the Fidelis crew came back to the trucks, the smell outside the restaurant was driving her nuts. With nothing to do but think of how badly she wanted a needle, a spoon, and a pancake, she closed her eyes and did her best to sleep, rehearsing what she would say when she saw her father:

"Father." *Don't think I've ever called him that before.* "I was wrong, and I know the things I did go against everything you and Momma taught me. I've disgraced myself and our family with the places I've gone and the things I've done, and I've wasted everything you gave me. I know I can never be your little girl again, but please don't let me starve. All I want is a job."

ani sat bolt upright, shaking cobwebs from her head and mumbling, "All I want is a job."

"Hey!" someone outside said. "There's someone in here! Care to explain this?"

A uniformed man holding a German Shepherd on a tight leash stepped down off the trailer and spoke into a radio, asking whoever was on the other end to send someone who spoke Spanish.

"What's the problem?" Greg sounded irate. "We're not even close to being over the weight limit."

"Hands on the truck! Save yourself and me some trouble. You carrying more of them or just this one?"

"What the…?"

Greg's son started to cry as the officer frisked his father.

"Sure, you're surprised," the officer said. "They all are. Any more surprises? We'll find the drugs easily enough, but I don't want to find a bunch of dead Mexicans in some secret compartment three days from now."

Another officer approached the GTO. "*Venga usted. Sal del auto, señorita.*"

"Dani? What the…?" Greg hollered over his shoulder. The officer cuffing him ordered him to be quiet. "She's Italian, you moron."

"Sure she is. We get Italians crossing the border all the time. Real problem these days."

Dani shook her head, nausea and darkness overtaking her as she tried to focus on the officer. "I'm not…"

Chapter Forty-One

Just after ten at night, Vic dragged himself into the office. He'd come to hate traveling but, he reasoned, you have to do what you have to do. *Finish up the paperwork. Check messages. Long as there isn't anything on the answering machine about the world burning down, I'll be in bed soon enough.*

Just three messages.

At 2:40 p.m.: "Hello, this is the California State Police. We have impounded two of your trucks and the ten vehicles they were carrying. We have found traces of drugs and an illegal immigrant. We need you to come to the State Police station…"

At 7:15 p.m.: "Vic, this is Dad. I've tried reaching you. Dani's in Saint Agnes Hospital in Fresno. Get there when you can. I'm going now."

At 9:30 p.m.: "Mr. Grassigli, this is the California State Police. We called earlier. There's been a mistake, and you've been cleared to claim your trucks, but we'll still need you to come to the station…"

Chapter Forty-Two

"She's waking up!"

Dani tried to blink the fog away. *Greg?*

The familiar cramps reminded her it had been too long since she'd had a hit. But were they fainter? Maybe just a little.

Voices she couldn't place fought for attention until Daddy's voice cut through from outside the room. As her vision started to clear, she made out another bed, empty, in the sterile room. A pair of nurses pushed their way past a uniformed police officer standing in the doorway.

The officer stepped aside as Daddy, in his wheelchair and wearing a red Marine Corps T-shirt, filled the doorway. With one turn of the wheels, he covered the distance between them and reached for her hand.

"Father," Dani said.

He recoiled, and she felt his hand tense on hers.

"Father," she repeated, choking out what she'd rehearsed through involuntary sobs, "I was wrong, and I know things I did go against everything you and Momma taught me."

He looked like he'd been slapped, his neck muscles tensing as his face turned red.

"I've disgraced myself and our family with the places I've gone and the things I've done."

Dani fought to stay awake, clearing her throat and doing her best to ignore the nurses poking, prodding, and checking everything from pulse to pupil dilation.

"I know I can never be your little girl again, but…"

Daddy softened his grip, grasping the bed rail with his free hand.

"Please don't let me starve."

Every vein in his neck and arm bulging, Daddy forced himself to a standing position, leaning over her.

Dani closed her eyes. "All I want is a job, Daddy. Please just let me work for you."

As she felt his lips brush against her forehead, she said, "You don't know the half of where I've been," and faded back into unconsciousness.

When Dani woke again, Daddy was the only one in the room, sitting on the corner of her hospital bed staring into her eyes as if he hadn't moved the whole time other than to sit. A different police officer stood just outside the doorway.

"Father," she started again, wondering how he'd answered the first time. "I was—"

Daddy leaned over, putting a finger to her lips.

"My little girl is alive."

"You don't know how much trouble—" Dani said.

"Lawyer's working on it."

Dani doubled over.

"I won't pretend you're not in serious trouble." Leaning in to cradle her, Daddy whispered in her ear as she struggled to stay awake. "But I'll do whatever it takes to get you the help you need. And whatever happens, you will always be my little girl."

Chapter Forty-Three

"I understand," Vic said as the Ford executive brought the phone call to a close. He'd taken the same call from General Motors that morning and from Chrysler yesterday. Too much negative press surrounding Dani's arrest and hospitalization, they all said. The national and local press was a deal breaker, they all said.

No wonder. Vic saw the headlines: "Rock Star Gets Special Treatment in Court System; Father has Deep Pockets."

They're not wrong.

Even if they were, there wasn't going to be a dealership.

All this while Dad was trying to talk him into mortgaging the business to pay Dani's legal fees.

Vic hurled his electric pencil sharpener across the room. He expected it to shatter, but it just smashed a hole in the drywall and fell with an unceremonious thud.

The phone rang again. *Probably Toyota calling to tell me I can't even have a foreign car dealership. Not that I'd ever ask.* He let the answering machine get it.

"Vic, Dad. Need to—"

"Yeah, Dad," Vic sighed, picking up. "I'm here."

Within an hour, Vic was calling around to find an apartment.

Dad had sold the house.

Chapter Forty-Four

Dani blinked through tears as they pulled up to the Fidelis parking lot in Daddy's Trans Am. She'd cried the whole way home, thankful that the wind whipping hair into her face masked her tears. Teddy Bear leaned forward from the back seat, licking the moisture from her cheek. As they rolled up, she could hear Whiteheart's "Unchain" blaring over a PA system.

Daddy's lawyer had worked out a bail arrangement. The number seemed insane, but somehow, Daddy had managed to come up with the money.

Now it looked like the whole world had shown up to see her come home.

Greg manned an open barbecue pit, jogging from one end, where he flipped ribeyes, to the other, where he slathered sauce over enough racks of ribs to feed an army.

The whole youth group was there, clapping as they waited for Dani to get out of the car.

It looked like her entire senior class was there. She didn't even know all their names. *Daddy must have just gone through the yearbook and invited everybody.*

Shelly stood, smiling, a baby on each hip.

There was Stoner, leaning against his friend's Chevette, drinking a Coke and trying not to look out of place.

Cal hung on the edge of the crowd, looking like he was trying not to be noticed.

Even Mr. Wilkins was there, though his attention was fixated on the adjoining lot.

Kari and Julie sat at a picnic table, sipping lemonade and laughing.

Kari flapped both hands over her head as the car drove up. Julie gave half a smile and a little wave.

"Daddy, this is too much." Dani turned the rearview mirror toward herself, doing her best to make herself look presentable. Despite the hollow cheekbones, she thought she was starting to look a little like herself. She tried not to smile. "Really, we could have just had pizza with Vic."

Daddy smiled.

At the party, Dani walked a fine line between grateful and exhausted. Everyone had questions.

"No," she told Kari, "we don't know what will happen at court yet, but the lawyer told Daddy he's pretty sure he can keep me out of jail if I complete a treatment program."

"There are lots of places you can get good help," Julie said.

"It's okay," Dani told Cal. "I know you can't control your brother."

"Doesn't it bother you that I just call you Stoner?" Dani said.

Stoner looked confused.

"I mean, I never even learned your name," she said.

"That is my name."

"I don't believe you."

"Only name my dad gave me. But if you want the rest of my name, it's Steve. Steve Stoner."

"Have you seen my dad?" Dani asked Shelly, handing a baby over.

"He was rolling around like he was on a mission a few minutes ago."

When the two of them were alone, Shelly looked away, holding her sleeping son. A tear splashed on her baby's head.

"I'm sorry," Shelly said. "I introduced you to all of it."

"Don't."

Dani scooted closer, laying her head on her friend's shoulder. The girls wiped one another's tears until their shaking woke the babies.

Chapter Forty-Five

Dad rolled into the office like an Abrams tank and yanked the phone cord out of the wall.

"What are you doing?" Vic said, adding an expletive. "Don't you know I'm trying to keep this business afloat? Bad enough you have all that racket going on outside!"

"You've been praying for this day for two years," Dad said, his voice low. "There's nothing going on in here so important you can't come out and celebrate with us."

"I can't."

A thunderous silence fell over the room as Dad looked him dead in the eyes.

"She drove this business into the ground, Dad. Everything you worked for."

"You two are what I worked for."

"Yeah, sure, Dad. Us two. Her, you mean."

Dad stiffened and barked, "Listen—"

"No, you listen. I have worked my tail off for you. Always have. Straight A's my whole life. If you said jump, I asked how high. I put my dreams on hold to keep your business going. How many parties did you ever throw me?"

"We've always—"

"Dad, since Dani's been born, I haven't even had a birthday party."

"You always had them—"

"Together. Yeah, I know. But let's get real. From the time she was born, they were all about Dani, right down to the flavor of the cake. Do you even know what kind I like?"

"German choco—"

"That's not the point!" Vic felt the veins in his neck bulging. "When's the last time you told me to invite friends over for a barbecue? I mean, all I did was walk the straight and narrow. No need to celebrate that, right? No, what we need to celebrate is coming home strung out. Come on, Dad, she's only here because she has nothing left. You were dead last on her list of choices."

The look on Dad's face tied Vic's gut in knots. *Not my fault. It's hers.*

"Son, everything I have has always been yours for the asking." Dad looked at the ground, making no attempt to stem the flow of tears. "But Dani was as good as dead, and now she's home. Celebrate with us."

"She's an addict," Vic said. "And she'll only use you again. Do you even know what people are saying about you because of that video?"

"She's my little girl."

"She's a whore."

"She's your little sister."

"Not anymore. You take her back if you want to. She's nothing to me. And she's not getting anything from this business."

Dad's face tinged pink, and it was clear he was making great effort to restrain his tone. "We were partners when you needed my name."

"Your name?" Vic screamed, wishing he had something to throw. "Our name isn't worth a plug nickel since Dani got done with it. You're a minority partner. And as long as I control the majority, not one red cent from this company is going to pay lawyers or treatment centers or any of that sort of thing. Finish your little party, and then I don't even want her on this property."

ad celebrated with Dani and her friends outside. It especially ground Vic's gears to see Julie and Kari having such a good time together. *They've both moved on from me. Dani's fault, like everything else.*

The hair on the back of his neck stood on end when he heard Dani laughing.

"At least she's going to go to jail where she belongs." Vic shook his head, realizing he was still arguing with his dad an hour after he'd slammed the door on the old man. "You've spent everything you have getting this far, and we both know you don't have the money to pay for any stupid treatment program."

"I'll find a way," he imagined Dad responding.

"Good luck with that."

The longer the party dragged on, the madder Vic grew. As the sun began to set, someone knocked.

"Go away."

Vic continued watching through the window, his stomach tied in knots. He rifled through his files, trying to occupy his mind with anything else. Ripping the file labeled "SERMON NOTES" from the folder, he threw it across the room, bouncing it off the rim of the wastepaper basket, papers filled with outlines fluttering around the room.

Screaming, Vic threw the outlines out, one by one, until his eye fell on the notes of a sermon he'd preached long ago and his own voice echoed in his brain:

"That brings us to the question. Are we our brother's keepers? Do we, like Cain, despise others because they're doing right when we know that we're not? Even if they're doing wrong, do we cast our brother aside? Or do we love one another? Do we protect one another, even when that means protecting someone from themselves? When we see our brothers doing something they shouldn't, do we restore them in love? Do we remember we could just as easily be the one who has fallen?"

Vic slammed his fists against the window frame.

Outside, Dad wore his brightest smile and waved as Mr. Wilkins sped off in his pristine '69 ½ Trans Am.

Song Credits

"Jump" by Van Halen; From the album "1984." Written by Michael Anthony / Alex Van Halen / Eddie Van Halen / David Lee Roth; © 1984 Warner Records Inc.

"Sweet Child O' Mine" by Guns N'Roses; From the album "Appetite for Destruction." Written by Guns N' Roses © 1987 UMG Recordings, Inc.

"My Lips Shall Praise You (Restorer of my Soul)" Written by Noël Richards and Tricia Richards; © 1991 Thankyou Music

"Another Crossroad" by Petra. From the album "Back to the Street." Written by Bob Hartman; © 1986 Star Song Music

"Wise Up" by Amy Grant; From the album "Unguarded." Written by Wayne Kilpatrick and Billy Simon; © 2007 Amy Grant Productions under exclusive license to Sparrow Records

"What a Way to Go" by Ray Kennedy, from the album "What a Way to Go." Written by Bobby David and Jim Rushing. © 1977 K-Tel

"Daring to Dream" Lyrics by Scott Rutherford and John Woolard; © 2019 Scott Rutherford and John Woolard

Bonus!

Free Download

"Daring to Dream"

Recorded by 1TK (River Music)

https://bit.ly/DaringtoDreamdownload

Made in the USA
Middletown, DE
01 October 2020